Birthright

Birthright

Zari

www.urbanbooks.net

Urban Books, LLC
300 Farmingdale Road, N.Y.-Route 109
Farmingdale, NY 11735

ISBN 13: 978-1-64556-731-8
EBOOK ISBN: 978-1-64556-735-6

First Trade Paperback Printing October 2025
Printed in the United States of America

10 9 8 7 6 5 4 3 2 1

This is a work of fiction. Any references or similarities to actual events, real people, living or dead, or to real locales are intended to give the novel a sense of reality. Any similarity in other names, characters, places, and incidents is entirely coincidental.

Distributed by Kensington Publishing Corp.
Submit Orders to:
Customer Service
400 Hahn Road
Westminster, MD 21157-4627
Phone: 1-800-733-3000
Fax: 1-800-659-2436

The authorized representative in the EU for product safety and compliance
Is eucomply OU, Parnu mnt 139b-14, Apt 123
Tallinn, Berlin 11317, hello@eucompliancepartner.com

Birthright

Zari

Chapter One

"I'm not gonna ask you again," J.R. Marx shouted as he slammed D'marco Heard's head into the bar. "Where the fuck is my fuckin' money?"

"I ain't got it!" D'marco finally shouted.

Nikki Marx walked up to D'marco and put her gun to his head. "Fuck you mean you ain't got it?"

"I can get it!" D'marco shouted. "I just need a couple of days, Nikki, I swear."

Nikki moved her gun away from D'marco's head, and J.R. allowed his body to slump to the floor. His face was a bloody and twisted mess. Nikki stood over him as he tried to get up. She put her foot on his chest when he got to one knee.

"Nobody told you to get up," she said, kicking him back to the floor.

J.R. looked around the packed spot. The name of the spot was Club XL, one of the nightclubs owned by Pete Barlowe for D'marco and his partner, Rashard Raymone. Rashard had seen Nikki and J.R. when they got out of their car. Once they armed themselves and went inside, Rashard knew he wanted no part of them or whatever they wanted, so he hid in the office.

"Where's snitchin'-ass, Rashard?" J.R. kicked D'marco in the face.

D'marco spit blood. "I ain't seen him," he lied quickly.

He knew Rashard was hiding in the office but feared it wouldn't go well for him if he told them that.

Nikki laughed. "Probably somewhere hiding from me." She walked over to the table where Andra Perry, Rashard's girlfriend, sat.

"Shit," Andra mumbled when she saw Nikki coming her way. "Hey, Nikki," she said when Nikki sat down at the table.

"Hey, Andra. Where's your nigga?"

"I swear I don't know where he is, Nikki," she lied. She'd seen Rashard when he hurried to the office to hide.

Nikki nodded. "I don't believe you." She stood up. "But it's cool. You tell him it's gonna be worse for him if I don't see him by the weekend."

Nikki walked away from the table and put her gun away. "Everybody in here needs to understand everything going on in those streets out there . . ." Nikki pointed toward the door. "It all belongs to me!"

When Nikki and J.R. left Club XL, everybody breathed a sigh of relief.

"That is one fine-ass nigga," Shekira Albertson said when J.R. left with Nikki. She was at Club XL with her best friend, Rasheda Saint James, who everybody called Rah-Rah.

"He is." Rah-Rah laughed. "Shame he doesn't know you exist."

"Yeah, well, I'm gonna change that soon. Mark my words. That is gonna be my man."

"In your dreams. What you gonna do with Sharonda Braelin?"

"That skinny, flat-chested bitch? Bitch, please. Once he gets hold of all these titties and this ass, he'll forget her name."

Rah-Rah laughed so hard she didn't notice that Tion Perkins had sat down at the table with them.

"What's up, Rah-Rah?"

"Wondering if you gonna buy me a drink or what?"

Tion chuckled and signaled for a server. He was a roadie for music video producer Levine Thatcher, and that was the only reason that Rah-Rah spoke to him. She was a dancer, or at least she wanted to be. She took ballet, tap, and African jazz from an early age and was a cheerleader in high school. In the years since then, Rah-Rah had been the lead dancer on several dance crews and had taken more dance classes to perfect her craft. When she and Shekira hit the clubs, Rah-Rah dominated the dance floor. She had even tried to make a break for herself when she danced at a strip club called the Platinum Club, where she heard that Thatcher had recruited a couple of girls who danced there to be in some of his videos. She didn't make it through the night because dancing was one thing; dancing naked for a bunch of men was more than she could handle.

When a server came to the table, Tion dropped a hundred-dollar bill on her tray. "Bring her whatever she wants."

Shekira folded her arms across her chest and frowned indigently. "She the only one you see sitting here?" she asked.

Tion looked at Shekira. "I didn't see you sitting there." He turned to the server. "Bring her what she's drinking too."

"What can I get you ladies?" the server asked.

"Henessy and Coke," Shekira said.

"Tequila Sunrise," Rah-Rah ordered. "Jose Cuervo gold, not the cheap shit," she said, and the server glanced at Tion. He nodded, and the server left to get the drinks.

Tion glanced at Rah-Rah. *She is so fuckin' sexy,* he thought as he looked deeply at the V-neck Xirena Axl twisted back tank that highlighted her abundant cleavage. He all but licked his lips.

"When you gonna let me take you out, Rah-Rah?" Tion asked, and she leaned closer to him.

"When you gonna get me in one of Levine Thatcher's music videos?"

"I told you. You need to come to one of Thatcher's auditions."

"Why I gotta do that? You've seen me dance a bunch of times. Right? You know how good I am."

"And she got that video dancer body," Shekira added. In addition to her abundant cleavage, Rah-Rah had the type of ass that made men want to follow her.

"I know, but that's the way it is. I could recommend you, but that would only get you in the audition," Tion said instead of admitting that he had no power, pull, or influence with Thatcher. His job was to set up and tear down the equipment. He doubted that his recommendation would carry any weight with Thatcher.

"I heard about them so-called auditions," Shekira said, shaking her head.

"Yeah, me, too," Rah-Rah co-signed.

"All you gotta do is get naked and fuck everybody, Rah-Rah, and you in there." Shekira laughed.

"Not gonna happen," Rah-Rah said to her best friend, but she wondered, if that's what it took, would she get naked and open her legs? "That's because my boy here is gonna hook me up," she said, caressing Tion's face gently.

When the server returned with the drinks, Tion got his change and stood up. He tossed a business card on the table in front of Rah-Rah.

"Call me when you get serious about wanting to dance, and we'll talk about that audition."

When he walked away from the table in search of new prey, Rah-Rah gave him the finger. "Fuck that nigga."

"At least he's good for drinks," Shekira said, but her mind was still on J.R. Marx and how she was going to get him to notice her.

As J.R. drove them away from Club XL, Nikki relaxed and made herself comfortable.

"What you wanna do now?" J.R. asked.

"Go by Marquee," Nikki said, and her younger brother headed for another club owned by Pete Barlowe.

"What you wanna go to Marquee for?" J.R. asked.

"Wesley owes me five grand, and he's been ducking me for weeks," Nikki said.

Nikki and J.R. Marx worked for Barlowe as his enforcers. The two had grown up in the game. Their father, Eddie Marx, started out with Barlowe. They built the formidable organization from an ounce of powder and, over the years, turned it into a very profitable drug, gambling, and prostitution operation.

Fifteen years ago, when Nikki was twelve and J.R. was only nine years old, their father was murdered. Nikki and J.R. were too young to know or understand what was happening at the time. At the funeral, Barlowe promised their mother, Naomi Marx, that he would take care of her and the children as if they were his own. Barlowe kept his word, and growing up, Nikki and J.R. wanted for nothing, and neither did their mother. They had the very best of everything.

"It's your legacy," Barlowe often told them growing up. "Your birthright." He taught them the game and how to survive in it.

As Nikki and J.R. matured into adulthood, they became more involved in the business and became Barlowe's enforcers. It was a job they gladly did because, as Barlowe himself often said, it was their legacy. And they were good at it. Barlowe's people feared the pair and especially thought that Nikki was ruthless. She didn't mind proving it. When you saw Nikki coming, you apologized and got in line, or she introduced you to the consequences.

Now they were no longer anxious teenagers. Nikki was twenty-four, and J.R. had just celebrated his twenty-first birthday. She was becoming increasingly dissatisfied with Barlowe and the way he treated them. It had gotten to the point where Nikki sometimes thought about killing Barlowe and taking what she felt was their birthright.

However, J.R. was entirely loyal to Barlowe and couldn't understand why, after all these years, his sister wasn't. To Nikki, the only good thing about their current position was that Barlowe paid them well, and he had taught them well. Nikki and J.R. were brutal, and they knew how to make money.

When they arrived at Marquee, Wesley Nelson, who sold heroin for Barlowe, was alerted that Nikki was in the place and was on her way to the office. He went to the safe in the office and got six thousand dollars before he closed it. The money was stacked neatly on the desk when Nikki and J.R. entered the office.

Nikki nodded when she saw the money on the desk. "That me?"

"It is. You're welcome to count it if you like."

Nikki picked up the money. "No need. You know better than to short me on my money," she said, took out her gun, and shot Wesley in the foot.

He screamed in pain. "What you do that for?"

"Fuck you think?" J.R. said, barely able to contain his laughter as Wesley hopped on one foot.

"Next time, don't make me have to wait for my money and have to come looking for you," Nikki said to Wesley, and J.R. followed her to the door.

"Stop screaming, nigga. You gonna live," J.R. said.

Nikki pointed her gun at his head. "Next time, you'll die for it," she said, leaving the office.

As J.R. drove them away from Marquee, Nikki looked at her brother and thought about telling him the truth. She had gotten tired of waiting for Barlowe to give her what she thought she was entitled to and had begun taking it. Without her brother or Barlowe's knowledge, Nikki had been taxing drug dealers and runners she knew were skimming, and she was thinking about doing the same thing with his gambling spots. What Nikki didn't know was that if she wasn't careful, things were about to come to a head and explode. She had more than her share of enemies who would like nothing more than to bring Nikki down.

Chapter Two

The nineties were booming. It was an excellent opportunity for two enterprising young men who were ready and willing to do what needed to be done to make money and were willing to get their hands dirty. Fast Eddie Marx and Pistol Pete Barlowe were two construction workers by day and small-time drug dealers by night. Both presented them with growth opportunities. As their drug business grew, they took some money and started a construction company. That got them a lot of work as subcontractors during the boom, and they made a lot of money.

The same was true for their drug business. Cocaine, marijuana, and heroin sales led them into gambling, prostitution, and other illegal activities, and by the turn of the century, the pair was both wealthy and powerful. Fast Eddie was a family man, happily married to Naomi, with two children, Nishelle and Eddie Junior. Pistol Pete was married as well, but it didn't make him any less of a ladies' man with a wandering eye. Over the years, he cheated on his wife, Caroline, relentlessly.

All of their lives changed the night that Fast Eddie was gunned down in the driveway of their house. At his funeral, Pete promised Naomi that not only would he avenge her husband's murder "At the hands of cowards," but he would take care of her and Eddie's children. His wife, Caroline, couldn't have any children of her own. Therefore, she treated young Nikki and J.R. as if they were her own children until the day she died from complications of ovarian cancer.

Following her father's murder, Nikki was angry, and her mother found her hard to reach. Pete saw that same angry young girl and decided to channel that anger, drive, and determination into business. He turned Nikki into a weapon. Where Eddie wanted his children not to be involved in his business, Pete taught Nikki and her impressionable younger brother the game. Naturally, they excelled, and now, they were his best enforcers, the ones he counted on when he needed something done and there was a point to be made.

That afternoon, in a seven-bedroom, ten-bath cul-de-sac home built on a full acre of land, Arya Cornelius walked into the foyer featuring a magnificent double staircase and Italian porcelain slabs. There was French oak wide-plank flooring throughout the house. She had spent the morning shopping at The Shops at Columbus Circle and had lunch at Mastro's Steakhouse. Once again, she had overspent the sizable allowance that Pete Barlowe gave her each month, but she didn't care about overspending because she had Barlowe wrapped around her little finger.

When he heard her come in, Pete left the library in his home, where he did the majority of his business and entertainment, and he went to greet her. He walked into the foyer and saw all her shopping bags.

"My God, woman," Barlowe said.

"What?"

"All of them bags." He walked up to her, shaking his head. "How much of my money did you spend today?"

"As much as it took for your woman to look good for you, baby." She kissed him.

"You look amazing all the time," he said to the beautiful young woman.

At thirty-seven years old, Arya was twenty-seven years younger than her man. She had played the other woman for years before Caroline passed away. *May she rest in peace.* Ten years later, it was Arya's time, and she was taking full advantage of the situation.

"You wouldn't be so worried about how much money I'm spending if you'd get your folks to stop skimming."

"Skimming?" Barlowe went to sit down. "Who's skimming?"

"Look, baby." Arya sat down next to him. "I'm just telling you what the talk is, and the talk is that it's the wild, wild west out there. Niggas is out there lawless getting money." She put her arms around his neck and kissed him on the cheek. "You know I hear shit that people wouldn't dare mention around you, lover."

"I know you do. Which is exactly why you need to tell me what you heard, and who you heard it from."

"Remy."

"Remy?" Barlowe questioned. Remington Sharp was his top seller.

"That's just what I heard. It may be just all talk."

"No, no, it makes sense."

The fact that Arya heard things that he needed to know was what had attracted Barlowe to her. He kept her around because Arya always knew what was going on and made sure that he knew about it. She had been his eyes and ears in the street; although nobody else did, he had come to trust her.

"That muthafucka always thought he was too big for his shoes. Wanting what I have."

"Like I said, that's just what I heard. Hear the nigga tell it, he's as honest and loyal as any of your soldiers."

"You asked him about it?"

"I might have mentioned a little something to him."

Barlowe grabbed her by the shoulders. "Fuck you do that for?"

"To put something on his mind," Arya said, even though she'd done no such thing. She hadn't heard anything about anybody skimming.

"Now the muthafucka will see me coming and put his house in order." He let her go.

"That doesn't mean you can't call J.R. and send him to have a talk with Remy," Arya suggested, more because she wanted to see J.R. than anything else.

"No, it doesn't," Barlow said and picked up the phone.

"What's up, Uncle Pete?"

"Grab your sister and come through. I need you to do something for me."

"On my way," J.R. promised.

J.R. gladly dragged himself out of bed.

"Where are you going?" his girlfriend, Sharonda Braelin, asked.

"I gotta go to work." J.R. put on his pants.

"But we were talking. Any time I have something to say, you gotta go."

"Yeah, well, it's like that sometimes."

"Not sometimes, J.R. All the time."

"Sorry."

"No, you're not. If you were sorry, if my feelings meant anything to you, you wouldn't run away when I have something to say."

"Maybe that's because you've said it all before, more than once, and it's gotten old."

Sharonda bounced out of bed. "Old? What's getting old is you constantly cheating on me."

"This shit again."

"Yes, this shit again. I am not a fool, you know. I know that every time you run away from me, it's not Uncle Pete calling.

"No, sometimes it's Nikki calling me to put in work."

"I'm tired of this shit!" Sharonda shouted.

"Look, Sharonda, I'm tired of it, too. So, I tell you what. Since you're tired of this shit, you don't need to be here when I get back," J.R. said, and he left the condo.

"Wait!" Sharonda shouted at the closed door.

Meanwhile, in another part of the city. There was something a little more intense going on.

He watched as she crawled onto the bed and elevated her ass in the air. He got up on his knees, spread her legs, and entered her with force. She bucked as hard as she could, slamming her wet pussy into him while he pounded her from behind. When she felt his body jerk, she tightened her muscles around him. He leaned forward, and his hands caressed her thighs and then her bouncing breasts. With a thrust of his hips, he shot his dick into her with so much intensity that she had to steady herself. He thrust himself into her again and again, and each time, it felt like he was going deeper than before. He grabbed her shoulders to hold her in place, and she gyrated her hips.

He began to move faster, and she began rocking her hips furiously, pounding her body into his until she had taken it all from him. He pushed himself as deeply and as hard into her as he could. She grabbed the back of his head, and he licked and sucked her nipple, all the while continuing to push himself inside her. Her head drifted back with her mouth open and eyes wide. He kept pushing it to her until she collapsed on his chest, but she didn't stop moving.

"That was so fuckin' good," he said and collapsed on the bed.

"Yeah."

Nikki sat up. She was done with him, and now it was time for him to go.

"You need to get dressed now and leave," Nikki said as she got out of bed.

She had met him the night before while she and J.R. were at the bar at Marquee after she had concluded her business. He was at the bar, drinking with friends. He wasn't bad looking, his hands and feet were big, and he talked a strong game. So, she decided to see if he had the dick game to match.

"It's like that?" he asked but got no answer.

Nikki walked into the bathroom and closed the door behind her.

"I guess it is," he said meekly and got out of bed. When he was dressed, he left the condo and walked into J.R. as he was about to ring the bell.

"What's up?" J.R. asked.

"Good luck with her," the man said with his head hanging low. He thought that he hadn't satisfied her and she had called someone else to finish the job.

"Nikki!" J.R. shouted before he used his key and went inside. "Nikki!"

She came out of the bedroom wearing a Kiki de Montparnasse floral lace robe. "Stop all that hollering. I heard you the first time."

"But you didn't answer." J.R. went into the kitchen and got a bottle of beer from the refrigerator. "So, I used the tracking on your phone." Both brother and sister agreed it was essential to always know where the other was at all times.

"What are you doing here anyway?"

"Get dressed. Uncle Pete wants to see us."

"He says why?"

"Nope. He just said, 'Grab your sister and come through. I need you to do something for me.'"

"Okay." Nikki headed for the bedroom. "I'll be ready in a few."

Once Nikk was dressed and ready to go, they left the condo that she barely came to these days. The only reason that she was there that day was to have sex, something else that Nikki didn't do a lot of these days. She had an itch that needed scratching. "He'll do," was the way she saw it.

Nikki didn't like coming to her condo because it held too many memories of her ex, Antawn. She and Antawn had been together for three years, and Nikki had fallen in love with him. He said that he loved her too, but it was the ideal situation for him. Antawn wasn't involved in the life. He worked a nine-to-five job as an associate marketing analyst. Keeping the hours that Nikki kept was perfect for him. Antawn saw Nikki when, and only when, she had time for him.

"I wanna see you," he would call to say.

"Not tonight. I have something I need to do. But I'll call when I'm done. If you're not busy, you can come through."

Antawn would come to her condo, and they'd have sex and maybe watch some television, but it was enough for Nikki, and she was happy in her relationship. That changed the day that she received a call from her girl-friend, Megan.

"I was passing your condo and saw Antawn going into the building with another woman."

"Thanks, Megan."

When Nikki got there, she went inside and heard them fucking. It broke her heart. Nikki took out her gun and placed it on her lap. When the woman came out of the bedroom naked, Nikki pointed the gun at her.

"Why don't you sit down," Nikki said to the naked and scared woman.

The woman put up her hands. "Please don't hurt me," she said and sat down across from Nikki.

"You can put your hands down," Nikki said, motioning with the gun.

"Thank you." The woman lowered her hands.

"How long have y'all been together?"

"Six months."

"I guess that he never told you about me, has he?"

"No, he hasn't said a word about you." She wanted to ask who Nikki was, but she still had a gun pointed at her.

"So, I know he never told you this is my condo, and I pay the mortgage."

"No."

"Call him. Tell him to come out here."

When he came out of the room and saw Nikki sitting there, he stopped in his tracks. "Oh, shit."

"Yeah, oh shit." Nikki turned to the woman. "You can go."

"Thank you," she said, hopping up and rushing into Nikki's bedroom to get her clothes.

While she was in the room, Nikki said nothing to Antawn. She sat there, pointing her gun at him and wondering how many other women he had brought to her condo.

Once she was dressed, the woman rushed to the door. "I'm sorry," she said and got out of there.

"I'm sorry, Nikki," he said.

"Crawl to me. Like the dog you are."

"I'm sorry, Nikki," he said as he crawled to her.

"Get out of my sight before I kill you."

It was the following day that Nikki went to the condo and found Antawn on the couch with another woman. He had not only been using her condo to have sex with other women, but he was also married.

"Nigga, please. Why are you even taking her side?" the woman asked, gathering her clothes and heading for the door. "That ain't even your wife."

Nikki was devastated by his betrayal. She thought about killing him on the spot, but he wasn't worth it; therefore, Nikki asked him to leave at gunpoint. He put up his hands and walked out of Nikki's life.

Not wanting to spend much time at her condo, she had been staying at her mother's house.

Chapter Three

When they arrived at the house, Barlowe ran down what he heard was going on without mentioning that he'd heard it from Arya. Nikki didn't trust her. Then he told them what he wanted them to do.

Nikki sat listening to Barlowe talk about his people skimming, and she did her best to look both surprised by the information and outraged that something like this could be happening on her watch. That was her brother's reaction, but the situation wasn't news to Nikki, since she was one of the ones skimming. She had known that some of Barlowe's top earners were skimming. She knew this business inside and out, and how much money could potentially be made. With that knowledge, Nikki imposed a tax on those individuals without J.R.'s, and indeed not Barlowe's, knowledge.

As she listened to Barlowe, Nikki had an idea. She glanced at J.R., deciding she would tell him about it later.

"We got it, Uncle Pete." J.R. bounced up from his seat.

"I knew you would," Barlowe said, looking at Nikki as she got up slowly. "I know I can always count on you two."

"We'll get Remy and them in line," J.R. said and walked out of the library.

Barlowe noticed that Nikki was quiet. "Everything all right, Nikki?" he asked.

She walked to the door and stopped to look back at Barlowe. "Everything is lovely."

Nikki had to laugh because Remy was the only one of his major earners who wasn't skimming off the top. That was because he was making so much money that he didn't see the need to skim. Like most people, Remy feared Nikki, and he hated J.R.

On the way to the home of Remington Sharp, Nikki sat quietly as J.R. drove and talked about what he thought about people skimming from Barlowe.

"Disloyal, thieving muthafuckas."

"Loyalty goes both ways. You can't do muthafuckas wrong and expect them to stay loyal to you. It don't work like that. Or at least it shouldn't."

"So, what is you saying? That Remy and them got a reason to be lying, thieving, disloyal muthafuckas, and it's okay?"

"No. That's not what I'm saying."

"What then?"

"I'm talking about us, J.R., you and me."

J.R. looked at Nikki strangely. "What are you talking about?"

"Nothing." Nikki was frustrated that he couldn't see that it was about them and that Barlowe wasn't doing right by them. So, she changed the subject. "Other than Remy, who else do you think Barlowe was talking about?"

"Remy, definitely. Brick . . . Dobie, Jackson, Paddington."

"Not Pad." Nikki was impressed, but she shouldn't have been. J.R. was right; Brick, Dobie, Jackson, and Paddington were the ones she was taxing for skimming. But J.R. knew enough about how their business worked and the people involved to know who was skimming. She had plans for Paddington, but she would talk to Brick, Jackson, and Dobie by herself.

"Yes, muthafuckin' Pad."

"Tell you what. When we got to Remy, it's your show," she said.

"Seriously?"

"Yeah. You handle it."

"Why? Did Uncle Pete say something to you about me?"

"No."

"Well, what then?"

"I wanna see if you can handle it, that's all. When it's all said and done, it's just you and me. We ain't got nothing but us we can depend on."

"That's not true. We can depend on Uncle Pete."

"No, we can't. He ain't family. He ain't really our uncle."

"You're wrong."

"No, little brother. You're wrong, and I wish I could get you to see it. I know when shit gets really fucked up, the only one coming to save my ass is you. And I'm good with that. Barlowe got his own agenda, and that's looking out for Pete Barlowe, first, last, and always."

"You sound like Mom now."

"That's because she knows Pete Barlowe much better than you and me ever will. She's right about him, and you need to listen to her." Both brother and sister got quiet. "Look, all I'm saying is I got your back when no one else will."

"And I got yours, always."

"Just remember that when shit goes south and it's just me and you."

When they arrived at Le Bistro Urbain, the New Orleans-themed French restaurant that served ratatouille, steak au poivre with red wine pan sauce, Marseille-style shrimp stew, and bouillabaisse where Remy did business, Nikki let J.R. take the lead as she had promised.

"Remy here?" J.R. asked the manager.

"He's in the office." She looked at him flirtatiously. "If you have a seat, I could let him know you wanna see him."

"That's fine. What's your name, cutie?"

"Ladonna. Ladonna Marco." She laughed. "But you knew that." She had been the manager at Le Bistro Urbain for years and enjoyed the flirtatious banter that she shared with J.R.

"Well, Ladonna Marco, I'm J.R. Would you please tell Remy that J.R. and Nikki Marx are here to see him?"

Ladonna nodded. "So, you're J.R. Marx."

"And you know this. Pimp, player, woman slayer." He chuckled.

"Whatever, J.R. Wait here," she said and walked away, swinging her hips because she knew J.R. was watching. She looked over her shoulder and smiled coyly before disappearing from sight.

"You and your women," Nikki said, shaking her head and sitting down to wait.

"What? I don't say shit to you about the men you're humping and dumping since you broke up with asshole Antawn, do I?"

Nikki laughed. "No, you don't."

"I can't help it if every woman wants to get with me."

"No, you can't. It's just different."

"What's the difference?"

"The difference is your women fall in love with you."

"I can't help that either."

"That dick is gonna be what gets you killed."

"Don't say that. Not even funny," J.R. said as Remy's woman, Francine Chaput, came through the door at Le Bistro Urbain.

"Oh," she said when their eyes met.

"You look nice," J.R. said at the sight of her in a Brunello Cucinelli precious net embroidery dress and Christian Louboutin So Me spike sandals.

"What are you doing here?" she asked quietly, looking around the near-empty restaurant.

"We're here to see Remy," J.R. said, and that was when Francine noticed Nikki was with him.

"Hey, Nikki."

"Hey, Francine."

"How are you doing?" she asked as Ladonna came out of the office with Remy and two of his men, Hakeem and Jace.

Francine quickly dropped her head and looked away from J.R. as Remy approached them.

"Sup, Nikki! Sup J.R.!" Remy all but shouted. He walked up to Francine, and she put her arm around his neck and kissed him.

"What's up?" J.R. said. "Somewhere we can talk?"

"Office." Remy pointed and took Francine's hand in his. He started for the office with Francine walking beside him and his men in tow.

"Alone."

Remy stopped and faced J.R.

"Somewhere me, you, and Nikki can talk alone."

Remy looked at Nikki. She smiled. He let go of Francine's hand. "Go get us a table. I'll be with you in a minute," he said to Francine, but he was looking at Nikki.

She nodded her head, and Remy watched as his men escorted her to a table. He turned to J.R. and Nikki and pointed.

"Office."

"Lead the way," J.R. said, and they followed him to his office. Once they were seated, Remy sat down behind his desk. "What's up?"

"Barlowe says that he knows some of your people are holding out on you. Skimming." J.R. held up his hands. "He says he doesn't think it's you, but he thinks you need to get your people to tighten up."

"This some bullshit, Nikki!" Remy protested.

Nikki held up her hands. "He's just telling you what the man said."

"This some bullshit!" Remy repeated, and then he tried to calm down. "So, what does *Mr. Barlowe* want me to do?"

"I already told you. *Mr. Barlowe* expects you to see that your people tighten up and come correct with his money."

"Anything else?"

"No. That's it."

"I need to talk to Nikki." Remy looked at J.R. "Alone," he said when J.R. didn't move.

J.R. nodded his head. "I'll be at the bar, Nikki." He stood up and left the office.

"What's up?" Nikki asked once the door closed.

"What is really going on?"

"What do you mean?"

"I mean, where this shit come from?"

"All I can tell you is this is where it is now. The man says we need to talk to you and everybody else about tightening up. I guess he thinks the money ain't right. I don't know. And you know I don't give a fuck."

Remy held up his hands. "You know what this seems like to me?"

"What does it seem like to you, Remy?"

"This seems like some of Arya's shit."

"You think that's what this is?" Nikki asked, but she agreed with him. It was her first thought when Barlowe told her what he wanted.

"I know it is," Remy said confidently.

"Bitch been in his ear, telling him what to think for a long time, so I wouldn't be surprised."

"Was she sitting there when he said it?" Remy laughed. "Because you know the bitch is a ventriloquist. I've sat there and saw her words coming out of his mouth many times."

Nikki laughed because she knew it was true. "She wasn't in the room when he said it, but she was home when we got there."

"That's what I think this shit is. That's all I'm saying."

"I'll keep my eyes and ears open."

"That's all I can ask." Remy paused and sat back in his chair. "Let me ask you something else."

"Go ahead."

"You ever think about what's gonna happen when Barlowe retires, or somebody retires him?"

"You making a suggestion?"

"No. I'm just asking you a question."

Since it was something that Nikki thought long and hard about every day, she nodded her head. "Yes, I think about the future," she admitted, wanting to see where he was going with this.

"If and when that happens, shit is gonna fall to you and me. And when that happens, we need to get along and work together."

"I think so, too," Nikki lied. She neither liked nor trusted Remy. "When it happens, I think you and I will be just fine, Remy. Me and you never had no problems."

"We haven't. But money and power always have a nasty habit of changing things."

"See that it doesn't do that to you," Nikki said. "I can assure you that I know exactly what I'm gonna do." Nikki paused for effect. "*If* and when Barlowe retires, or somebody retires him."

Meanwhile, out in the restaurant, J.R. sat down at the bar to wait for Nikki to finish talking to Remy. Francine was sitting at a table nearby with Remy's men. She pushed her lips together and blew him a kiss. He winked at her and looked away. It was right about then that two women walked by the table where Francine and Remy's men were sitting.

"What's your rush, sexy?" one of his men said and grabbed one woman by the hand.

When the two women stopped to talk, Francine stood up. "I'm going to the ladies' room," she said and walked away from the table.

When J.R. turned and saw her, Francine discreetly pointed toward the restroom. He looked at Remy's men. They were all into the women they were talking to and not paying attention to him and Francine. *And why should they?* J.R. and Francine had always been discreet about their yearlong affair.

He got up and went toward the restroom. Francine was standing outside the ladies' room when he got there.

"Hey."

"Hey, yourself."

Francine pushed open the door to the men's room. "Hello!" When she didn't get an answer, she grabbed J.R. by the hand and pulled him in.

"What are you doing?" J.R. asked, but he knew what she wanted.

"Shhh." Francine placed her finger against his lips.

He kissed her finger and complied with her wishes. Francine leaned forward and looked under the stalls. Not seeing any feet, she opened one stall, led him into it, and closed the door.

J.R. leaned forward and kissed her. Francine moved closer to him, and he put his arms around her. They kissed again. He enjoyed the feeling of sheer ecstasy as her hands explored his body, and it made his dick stiffen. His nipples got harder, and his body ached to feel her tongue against them. His nipples were his weakness. Francine knew it, and she had every intention of exploiting that fact. She wanted J.R. to be weak for her, just like she was weak for him. As they got caught up in the moment, Francine gathered her Brunello Cucinelli dress around her waist.

She broke their embrace and turned around. Before J.R. could wrap his arms around her waist, Francine held on to the stall wall with one hand, gingerly put her feet on the commode, and stepped up. She had to hold the walls to balance herself, but once she had, Francine bent her knee to take him into her warmth.

J.R. stepped up, stroked his erection, got behind her, grabbed her hips, and entered her. Her pussy was so wet, and his dick was so hard that he began to pump it in her as hard as he could.

"Give it to me harder. I wanna feel all of that dick in me."

"Shhh."

He reached for her shoulders, pounded his dick into her, and felt her cum again. The feeling of her spasming pussy around his dick felt so amazing to him that he felt himself about to cum and had to force himself to slow down. He knew he didn't have much time, but he still wanted to make it last.

J.R. grabbed her ass and ran his hands up and down her back and across her cheeks, and she started to move her hips faster. He felt her body begin to shake. She moved her body up and down on him, grinding her hips into him with each stroke. J.R. felt his dick expand, and he pushed it to her harder. As she drenched him with her juices, he slid his hands from her shoulders down her back, and then he gripped her beautiful, firm ass.

J.R. began to feel her legs trembling on his thighs, and he pushed harder. Francine bore down on him and increased her pace. She started pounding her hips furiously onto him until she reached a very violent climax.

When it was over, both quickly fixed their clothes and came out of the stall. J.R. went to the door and looked out into the hallway. He kissed her on the cheek.

"You go ahead."

"Call me," Francine said and left the men's room.

J.R. waited until she was gone before he came out and returned to the bar. When he got there, Nikki was waiting for him. She stood up.

"You ready?"

"Yup," J.R. said and followed Nikki out of Le Bistro Urbain. "What Remy want?"

"I'll tell you when we get in the car."

Chapter Four

"So, what did Remy wanna talk about?" J.R. asked as soon as they got in the car.

"Nothing that I hadn't been thinking about."

"What?"

"See, that's the thing, little brother. I don't know if I can talk to you about it."

"That's fucked up, Nikki. You can talk to Remy about it, but you can't talk to me?"

"Yeah, J.R., I know it was real fucked up. Whenever I try to talk to you about it, you get all excited and defensive."

J.R. took a breath and tried to calm himself. "I promise to hear you out and not say a thing."

"Okay. Remy asked me if I thought about what's gonna happen when Barlowe retires. Or somebody retires him."

"You think he's planning to make a move?"

"That's what I asked him."

"And?"

"He says he ain't."

"You believe him?"

"For the time being. But he bears watching. What he was talking about was him working with us when Barlowe retires. Or somebody retires him."

"I can see that." J.R. looked confused. "Why do you think I would get excited about that?"

"Because what you've been thinking about is now, but I've been thinking about and planning for the future. Our future. You and me. I know we're doing good. Never wanted for a damn thing."

"We're living well, always have, doing what we do," J.R. said, and Nikki pointed to his chest.

"Doing what *your* Uncle Pete taught us to do. He raised us to be his pit bulls. To savagely go after any and everybody he pointed us at. But I think we deserve more. That we're entitled to more. It's our birthright."

"You sound like Mom."

"Well, Mom is right. Barlowe didn't build this business by himself. Him and Daddy started the construction company and all them other legit businesses, and they made all that money together. The two of them. It was not just Barlowe that built the dope and gambling game."

"You're right."

"I know I'm right. And when Daddy got murdered, yeah, he took care of us and Mom, but that's it. He took care of us when we should be his partners in everything."

"So, what you gonna do? Because I know if you've been thinking about it that you have a plan. You already know what you're going to do." J.R. chuckled. "Shit, you may have already put your plan in motion and working on it right now."

Nikki laughed. "You know me too well."

"All my life. So, what's up?"

"So, first of all, and I hate I got to even ask this question, but who you with?"

"What you mean?"

"Are you gonna be all in with me, or you gonna give me some shit about us staying loyal to your Uncle Pete because he's been so good to us little children?"

"I'm with you. One hundred percent."

"All right. We're not gonna wait for him to give us what we're entitled to. We're gonna take the shit right out from under his nose without him even knowing it."

"I'm with you. How are we gonna do that?"

"He already laid the groundwork for it. Check it out," she said, and then told J.R. about her idea. "What we doing right now?"

"He got us going around to all his people to tell them they need to tighten up on the money."

"Right. And when the shit don't happen like he thinks it should, who's he gonna call?"

"You and me."

"Right. I'm gonna tell him that if me and you gonna be responsible, then we need to run it our way."

"That makes sense."

"As long as we keep the money flowing to him like it's been, he's not gonna pay any attention to how the money gets made, just that he gets his cut."

J.R. chuckled. "That's damn near how it is now."

"See what I'm saying? We can do this shit, and he not even know what's up."

"What about the connection?"

"Don't worry about that. I got that handled when the time comes."

Nikki had met Barlowe's Colombian connection, or at least she thought she had, on a trip to Los Angeles. She was at a party, and she met Luis de Jesus Castillo. He never came right out and said that he was the connection, but he knew who she was without being introduced. He knew Barlowe, and he knew her father. He even asked about her mother. They had a very long talk that ended with him giving her his number and saying that if she ever needed anything at all, all she had to do was call him, and it would be taken care of.

"But that's not something we have to worry about now because we're not making a move. Like Remy said, we gonna let Barlowe retire or wait until somebody retires him." Nikki raised her right hand. "I promise you that I will not take any action against him. I ain't that ungrateful a muthafucka. I just wanna take what should be ours."

"I'm good with that. Where do you start?"

"Roll us by Paddington's spot," Nikki said, and J.R. drove them to Mr. Vee's sports bar and grill. When their father and Barlowe had begun to branch out, Mr. Vee's was the first spot they bought. It was only fitting that Nikki and J.R. would start reclaiming their birthright there.

"Call Cairo and Butch and tell them to meet us there," she said, and J.R. called his boys.

When Eddie and Barlowe bought the spot from Peggy Vantaggiato after her husband died under mysterious circumstances, it was just a little dinky bar with a restaurant and a couple of T.V.s. Being in the construction business and knowing who to bribe came in handy. They renovated the spot and added a back room, where they began running a private gambling room. The place had been making money ever since. It was currently being run by Raahim Paddington. In addition to running the Palace, Pad, as he was called, sold heroin and cocaine for Barlowe. He was one of the ones that Nikki knew was skimming, and she was taxing him heavily for the privilege.

When Nikki and J.R. arrived at Mr. Vee's sports bar and grill, Cairo and Butch were already there waiting. The four went straight back to the gambling room, presented themselves to security, and were admitted. Nikki looked around for Paddington.

"You see him?" J.R. asked.

"No. Let's go to the office." Nikki started walking. "Back my play."

"What you gonna do?"

"I already told you. I'm taking this spot," she said and walked faster to the office.

J.R. leaned close to Cairo and Butch. "Be ready for anything. Nikki's going hard at them."

When they got to the office door, security smiled, said, "What's up, Nikki?" and opened the door for her. She walked right into the office. Paddington was caught a little off guard, mostly because he wasn't expecting to see Nikki that night. And she never came with J.R., so this was out of the ordinary. He was in there with two of his men, Isaac Christopher and Elijah Alexander.

"What's up, Nikki?" Paddington said as Nikki took a seat in front of his desk. "I wasn't expecting you tonight, or I would have had you set up and ready."

"No worries. We're about to come to a new understanding anyway."

"What's that?"

"You're out. You work for me now."

"Fuck you mean? I'm out, and I work for you now?"

"It's simple. I'm taking over this place. So, you can either work for me, or you can get the fuck on. Your choice."

"Fuck you and fuck that stupid shit you talking, Nikki. I ain't going no damn where, and if you think you can just walk in here and push me out, you're out of your mind. You got a lot of fuckin' nerve trying this shit on me, especially the way you're rolling."

"What's that supposed to mean?" J.R. asked.

"What Barlowe say about this?"

"He said you're out." Nikki took out her gun and shot Paddington in the head.

When he slumped in the chair, Isaac Christopher started to go for his gun, but Cairo shot him twice in the chest. J.R. pulled his gun and pointed it at Elijah Alexander. He quickly raised his hands.

J.R. took Alexander's gun. "Who you work for?"

"I work for Nikki now."

"Good," Nikki said and stood up. She went behind the desk and dumped Paddington out of the chair. "Until I say different, this is your spot now, Elijah. Can you handle it?" Nikki asked.

"Yeah, I can handle it."

"Then this is your chair now." Nikki turned the chair toward him. "Come on and sit down."

Alexander went behind the desk, got a handkerchief, and wiped away the blood before he sat down.

"How does it feel to be the boss?" J.R. asked.

"It feels good," Alexander said. Although he had worked for Paddington and was loyal to him, he hated his guts and was glad he was dead.

J.R. put his gun to Alexander's head. "Fuck up, and the same shit happened to Pad will happen to you. Understand?"

"I understand." He looked at Nikki. "You can trust me, Nikki. I won't betray you. You have my word."

"You know what will happen if you do," Nikki said. "You know my deal with Paddington?"

"I do."

"That ain't changed. You have that ready for me when I come back on Friday."

"You got it, Nikki."

"Call the cleaner," Nikki ordered. "Have him come take care of the bodies."

"I've got people here that can take care of that."

"No! I told you to call the cleaner."

J.R. returned his gun to Alexander's head. "Part of staying alive means that you don't ask questions. You do what you're told."

"Okay, okay," Alexander said with his hands up.

"When I tell you to do something and do it a certain way, there's a reason." Nikki sat down in front of the desk. "I want you to call the cleaner because the bodies need to disappear and not have your crew just dump the body somewhere for the cops to find. Do you understand?"

"I understand." Alexander picked up the phone to make the call.

"I know you want to get them outta your new office right away, but be patient. Do shit my way, and you will be rewarded for your loyalty."

"I got you, Nikki." Alexander stood up and raised his right hand. "I solemnly swear to you, Nikki, on the souls of my children, that I will always be loyal to you and do whatever you say."

She stood up. "I know you do."

Nikki left the Palace that night satisfied with her decision to kill Paddington, but she wasn't sure about Alexander. He had worked for Pad for years, and his loyalty to him was unquestioned. But the more Nikki thought about it, the more she understood that if she was going to make this work, she would need to have people she trusted in critical positions.

Chapter Five

"That's exactly why you need to let me run this my way," Nikki said when she laid out her plan for Barlowe. She decided it was better for him to hand her the power she wanted instead of taking it. "You want me to be responsible. That's what you used to say. 'Nikki,' you'd say, 'all this is for you and brother.' Or was that just some bullshit you say to kids to keep them in line?"

"No, Nikki. I meant every word of that. One day, all this will belong to you and J.R."

"Then let me run my show my way. That's all I'm asking."

"You sure you can handle it?"

"Yes, Uncle Pete," she said. "I can handle it."

"What about J.R.? You sure he's ready for this? Your brother can be a loose cannon sometimes."

"More like the bull in the china shop," Arya commented, and both Nikki and Barlowe just looked at her.

"I can handle J.R."

Barlowe chucked. "You ever notice that you only call me Uncle Pete when you want something?"

"No. I hadn't noticed that."

Arya rolled her eyes and looked away. "I have," she commented to more stares from Nikki and Barlowe.

"I don't know, Nikki. Shit's been working, and it's been working well for years. Why change it now? You know what they say: if it ain't broke, don't fix it."

"It's a new day. Give me a chance to do it my way, and I promise you that I will increase your revenue from the gambling, the women, the extortion rackets. Everything."

That was really all that he needed to hear. Barlowe sat there looking at Nikki for what seemed like a long time. He had to ask himself, was it all bullshit that he dished out like ice cream to kids, or was he serious? All that he had was at stake, so he had to get this right. If he wanted to be honest with himself, that rarely happened at times like this, but if it were to happen, Barlowe would have to acknowledge to Nikki that he didn't build the business by himself. In that moment of honesty, he would admit that it was Eddie Marx's vision of the future that he was living.

"I know you must have some other ideas about ways we can make this money. And I respect that, I do. But this here shit, this about what we gonna do to build this empire. It will make that other shit easier to get done when we're stronger," Nikki said.

Barlowe knew it was Eddie who had run everything, and he just went along for the ride. "Okay, Nikki. We'll try it your way. But I need to know what you're doing every step of the way. You need to talk to me every day and let me know what you're doing. Understand?"

"Understood." Nikki stood up. "I'm gonna show you, Uncle Pete." Some part of her felt like the young girl who was anxious to impress her Uncle Pete. This was her time now, and Nikki planned to make the most of it.

The Palace was another nightclub owned by Barlowe. It was the jewel of his entertainment enterprises. It was the largest of the clubs they owned, and it featured live performances and a four-star restaurant. According to their mother, the Palace was her father's pride and joy. While Pete ran the construction company, Eddie spearheaded their entry into the entertainment business because the clubs were a natural front for their gambling and drug operations. Now that she had the green light for her plan, it was only natural that Nikki would begin her rise to power there.

The Palace was run by Garrett Wilson. When Eddie was murdered, he was the one Barlowe put in place to run the spot. He had been there ever since. He didn't like Nikki, and he never had. He thought that she was a spoiled brat who needed a good beating. He thought that J.R. was out of control and irresponsible, and he was dangerous because of it. Now, he feared them both because they were a threat to his power. In addition to running the Palace, Wilson had his hands in everything, and his O.G. status caused him to ignore Nikki.

Those days were over.

That night, the Palace was also the destination for Shekira Albertson and Rasheda Saint James as well. Shekira heard that J.R. liked to hang out there, and she had decided that this would be the night she would make him notice her.

It was after one in the morning, and Shekira was starting to think that J.R. wasn't gonna show up there that night. She and Rah-Rah had been there since happy hour and sat through the first show, and there was no sign of J.R. She was excited earlier in the evening when she saw Sharonda Braelin, J.R.'s girlfriend, come into the Palace to be seated at a reserved table, but she left when the show was over.

Shekira was about to tell Rah-Rah that she was ready to go when J.R. walked in with Nikki, Cairo, and Butch. "There he is," Shekira said excitedly.

"Okay, he's here now. What are you gonna do?"

She sat there watching—craving, actually—as the four walked through the crowded club to the office. Cairo knocked on the office door, and she watched them go in.

***

"What's up, Mr. Wilson?" J.R. asked when he walked into the office.

"J.R., Nikki." Wilson sat up straight in his chair. "What can I do for you two?"

"Today, it's what I can do for you," Nikki said and sat on the edge of the desk.

"What's that?" J.R. sat in the chair in front of the desk and put his feet up.

"Boy, if you don't get your feet off my muthafuckin' desk."

"What you gonna do?"

"You need to check your brother, Nikki."

"I ain't here for that. I'm here to tell you that I'm giving you a chance to spend more time with . . ." Nikki snapped her fingers. "What's her name?"

"Mykisha Mystelle," Butch said.

"Right." Nikki laughed. "What kind of fuckin' name is that anyway?"

"The kind you make up." J.R. laughed.

"What the fuck are you talking about, Nikki?" Wilson demanded to know.

"You're out. I run this place now," she said boldly.

There was silence in the room. Wilson nodded his head as if he were resolved to his fate, and then he started laughing, loud and hardy.

"I heard about the stunt you pulled at Vee's the other night. That shit may have worked on Paddington's weak muthafuckin' ass, but I'm muthafuckin' Garrett Wilson!" he said, pounding his chest. "I was running shit in this town when you two were still sucking milk from your mama's titty. You got a lot of nerve thinking you can just walk in here and push me out."

"Who's gonna stop me?"

Once again, there was silence in the room.

"We'll see what Barlowe got to say about this," he said.

"I'm in a good mood tonight, so go ahead, call him. Because at this point, right here, right now, you got two choices. Either you get up from that chair and go home safe and happy, or you disappear. Your choice."

Wilson confidently picked up the phone, and with the call on speaker, he dialed Barlowe's number. "Put a stop to this shit right fuckin' now."

"G-Man! What's up?" Barlowe answered.

"Listen. I got Nikki here, talking out her ass about me being out." Wilson looked at Nikki. She had her gun out and pointed at his head.

"She's not talking outta her ass. If she says you're out, then you're out. Simple as that."

"But—"

"I'm in the middle of something, G-Man, so if that's all you wanted, I'll talk to you later," Barlowe said and hung up the phone.

"What's it gonna be?" Nikki cocked the hammer.

"Just like that?"

"Just like that," J.R. said.

Wilson looked at the four people in front of him and wondered if he could get his gun out of the drawer and shoot them before they killed him.

Probably not.

He thought for a second about whether that was how he wanted to go out. In a blaze of glory!

Probably not.

"I worked too hard to just walk outta here empty-handed," Wilson said humbly.

"So," J.R. said.

"I tell you what. You had a good night here tonight. I'm gonna let you walk away with all the money they made on the door tonight. That sound fair to you?"

"Yeah, Nikki." Wilson stood up and raised his hands. "I'm gonna get my gun from the drawer."

"Get his gun, Cairo. Then you escort him to the cash room to get his money, and then you can escort him to his car. You can give him back his gun then."

"Let's go," Cairo said once he had Wilson's gun.

"Go with him, Butchie," Nikki said and went behind the desk. She sat down in the chair.

"How does it feel?" J.R. asked.

"Like I need to get a new chair."

Meanwhile, out in the club, Shekira watched the office door like a hawk and saw Cairo and Butch come out with Wilson. She figured that it wouldn't be long before he came out.

"Come on," she said to Rah-Rah.

"Where we going?"

"To the bar." Shekira stood up. "Now, come on."

Dressed in Christian Louboutin duvette spikes leather and suede pumps and an Area halter-neck minidress with spaghetti straps and a star cut-out in the front that exposed her abundant cleavage, Shekira posted up at the bar, where she was sure that he would see her when he came out of the office.

"What can I get you ladies?"

"Henessy and Coke," Shekira said.

"Jose Cuervo gold Tequila Sunrise," Rah-Rah ordered, and that was when she saw Tion.

He was at the bar, standing next to Levine Thatcher. She waved when she saw him. Tion nodded to acknowledge her, and then Rah-Rah watched as Thatcher pointed to her and asked Tion something. Thatcher nodded, and before she knew it, they were coming her way.

"Here they come," Rah-Rah said breathlessly.

"What's up, Rah-Rah?"

"How you doing, Tion?"

"This is the woman I've been telling you about, Thatch. This is Rasheda Saint James. This is Levine Thatcher."

When Rah-Rah held out her hand, Thatcher bowed at the waist and kissed her hand.

"It's a pleasure to meet you, Ms. Saint James."

"It's a pleasure to meet you. And please call me Rah-Rah."

"Okay, Rah-Rah. May I sit?"

"Please."

"Thank you." Thatcher sat down and leaned close to Rah-Rah. "Tion tells me that you're interested in being in one of my music videos."

"Yes. Very interested."

"Well, let's talk about that," Thatcher said, holding out his hand.

Rah-Rah accepted his hand, stood up, and looked at Shekira. "I'll call you tomorrow," she said and left the Palace with Tion and Thatcher.

Shekira watched Rah-Rah until she was out the door, hoping that she'd be all right and wondering if she should have gone with her. When she turned back to the bar, J.R. was standing next to her.

"Hi."

He turned and looked at her, and his eyes focused on her exposed cleavage. "How are *you* doing?"

"You're J.R. Marx, right?"

"That's me."

"I heard a lot about you."

"What have you heard?"

"I heard a lot of good stuff about you." Shekita had been drinking Hennessy since happy hour, and by that time, all of her inhibitions were long gone. "And I wanted to know if there was any left for a sister like me?"

J.R. shot his drink, and then he looked her up and down from the tips of her Christian Louboutin pumps up to her thick thighs, to her abundant cleavage, to her pouty lips.

"Let's get outta here and go somewhere you can get all you want."

Chapter Six

It started out simple—but it always does—a couple of bumps of cocaine with champagne in the back of the limousine with Thatcher. He was listening to the new track from Dramatic, whose video he was casting dancers for. With the champagne glass in hand, Rah-Rah showed Thatcher a little of what she could do as they rode to his hotel. He had the penthouse and terrace suite at the Roxy hotel.

"Make yourself comfortable," Thatcher said, taking off his jacket and loosening his tie when they got to the suite.

"Thank you."

Rah-Rah walked into the room and looked around. The first things she noticed were the floor-to-ceiling windows and the rooftop terrace. She immediately went out onto the terrace and looked out at the spectacular view of the city below.

Thatcher walked up behind her. He liked bringing women there because the view always made them wet. "What are you drinking?" he asked.

"Tequila Sunrise."

"How about Tequila and orange juice?" He chuckled as he went to the mini bar. "Ain't no grenadine."

"That's fine."

Thatcher took his phone out of his pocket and put on another of Dramatic's songs. "Let me see what you got."

Rah-Rah started to dance. Thatcher handed her the drink and sat down to watch. He sipped his drink and nodded while he watched. She was good, and more importantly to Thatcher, Rah-Rah looked good in the Lilac Liv Foster asymmetric-hem studded dress that she got on sale to wear for the night. He couldn't wait to get her out of it. When the song ended, Rah-Rah started to come to sit down, but Thatcher had other ideas.

"Keep dancing."

She giggled. "There's no music."

"Right. Close your eyes and dance to the music in your mind," he said, getting up. He went to the bar and started another song on his phone. Then he went to get his jacket and got the bag of cocaine from his pocket before he returned to the couch. He emptied the bag and made a few lines.

"You wanna hit this?"

"Yeah."

Rah-Rah danced her way to the couch. She crouched at the table to the music, did the line, and came back up dancing.

"You got some skills."

"Thank you."

"I may just be able to use you."

"Really?"

"Yes." Thatcher did a line. "Really."

"That's great."

"Yeah." He nodded greedily. "Now, show me sexy and seductive," he said just as there was a knock at the door. "You keep dancing," Thatcher said, getting up to answer the door. "What's up?"

"I got two rocky sacks just for you."

"Just what the doctor ordered," Thatcher said and paid the man for the two eightballs of rocks.

He saw Rah-Rah dancing. "She's gonna be fun."

"They always are," Thatcher said and closed the door.

While Rah-Rah continued to dance, he walked into the bedroom. Thatcher got a box from the drawer and returned to the living area. He opened the box that contained two handheld glass pipes. Rah-Rah stopped dancing and stood over the coffee table in the suite.

"I've never seen a pipe like that before."

"It's called the Steamroller." Thatcher emptied the bag of rocks into the pipe box and got the lighter. He put a piece on and lit the pipe.

"You wanna hit?"

"Sure," Rah-Rah said, even though she had never smoked cocaine before. She coughed.

Thatcher laughed. "Let me get you another drink," he said, getting up to go to the bar.

"Thank you." Rah-Rah fanned herself. "It's getting hot in here."

He handed her the drink. "Why don't you show me your best combination move?"

While Rah-Rah did what she thought were her best dance moves, Thatcher returned to the couch and put another piece on the pipe. He lit up.

"You're right. It is getting hot in here." He unbuttoned his shirt.

"It's getting hot in here, so take off all your clothes." Rah-Rah sang the words to Nelly's song.

"If you want to."

Rah-Rah laughed and finished her drink. She danced to the bar. "You mind?" she asked, pointing to the mini bar in the room.

"Help yourself." While Rah-Rah danced, shook her ass, and fixed a drink, Thatcher got another hit ready. "You want another hit?"

"Sure."

Rah-Rah danced to the couch and sat down next to Thatcher. She shot her drink, and he handed her the pipe.

"Whew," she said and got up.

"This the song for the video coming on. Let me set the scene. All the dancers have on sexy lingerie, and Dramatic is looking over them, and then he gets to you, and you dance for him. Can you do that?"

"I sure can," Rah-Rah said and was about to start dancing.

"Wait." Thatcher looked her up and down. "What do you have on under that dress?"

Rah-Rah froze. "Just my bra and panties. Why?"

"Do you mind?"

"Mind what?"

"Taking off your dress. You're not shy, are you? This ain't no business for no shy girls."

"No, I'm not shy," she said and stripped down to her Le Mystere lace allure bra and panties.

"Good." Thatcher returned to the couch. "Show me what you got."

While Thatcher looked on, Rah-Rah danced to that and two more songs before he let her stop. He handed her the pipe, and Rah-Rah took a hit.

"You're burning it too hot."

"I'm sorry," Rah-Rah said and handed Thatcher back the pipe.

"You've never done this before, have you?"

"No, I haven't."

"That's all right." Thatcher picked up a cool pipe and put another piece on. "Close your eyes." He got it started, and while still holding the smoke in, he said, "Listen to the sound of my voice and pull it the way I tell you."

"Okay."

He put the tip of the pipe against Rah-Rah's lips. "Pull lightly."

Rah-Rah began to inhale the smoke.

"Good."

She took in some more smoke.

"Pull even," he said while he held the lighter to the stem. "Pull harder."

Those were the only words Rah-Rah heard until Thatcher moved the pipe away from her lips.

"You're right. That did make the high more intense," Rah-Rah said.

After a while, clothes came off, and they spent the rest of the night smoking until there was no more. Thatcher called for more; however, while they waited, they had sex. There was no passion involved. At least, not for Rah-Rah. But one thing was certain: by the end of the night, Rah-Rah was hooked. She was going to be in a music video, but she was hooked.

J.R. and Shekira went to Moxy on West 28th Street. When they got to the room, she offered to make their drinks. J.R. made himself comfortable on the bed.

"Go ahead."

She went to the mini bar and got two bottles of Hennessy. She was nervous, so she poured one and drank it straight down before making another drink with ice and Coke and making a drink for him. Shekira brought them the drinks and got comfortable on the bed next to him. They were lying on the bed, staring into each other's eyes, when his phone rang.

J.R. took out his phone and glanced at the display. "I have to take this." He got up and left the room.

"I'll be waiting, so don't be long."

"I won't be."

J.R. went and took his call, but when he came back to the room, she was asleep.

"Oh, no, she didn't. Ain't that a bitch." He shook his head and began to get undressed, then got in the shower.

Then he covered her up, got into the bed, and went to sleep.

In the morning, she was still asleep when he woke up. He got out of bed and went out on the balcony to make some calls. He was considering ordering room service when Shekira came out onto the balcony.

"Good morning," she said and sat in the chair beside him.

J.R. looked over at her, shook his head, and chuckled. "Morning."

"Sorry about last night. I guess I fell asleep on you."

J.R. nodded. "Yeah, you did."

Shekira moved closer. "Let me make it up to you." She stroked J.R.'s hard dick. "My pussy is so swollen and dripping wet. I need you to fuck me." Shekira squatted down in front of him, hurrying to reveal his dick.

"Huh," he groaned out as if he were in pain when she freed him.

Shekira took him into her hot mouth and began slobbering all over it. He palmed her head as Shekira worked back and forth, squeezing his balls before placing them into her mouth. She sucked gently on them as her hand continued to jerk him off. Shekira took J.R. into her mouth. He pumped in and out of her mouth, grabbing her head with both hands. When he felt like he was about to cum in her mouth, J.R. pulled her up.

"Come on," he said, grabbing her by the hand and all but dragging her into the suite. She took off her clothes and got on the bed as J.R. watched.

"Damn, you're fine as fuck." He got undressed quickly while Shekira fingered her wet pussy for his watching eyes. J.R. pulled out a rubber and covered himself, and then he joined her in bed. He spread her legs open and moved in between her thighs. J.R. entered her slowly and gently, making her back arch.

"Fuck me good," she said once his entire length was buried deep inside her.

"I will."

Shekira quickly wrapped her legs around his waist, and he stroked her pussy with that long, hard dick, with slow and constant strokes. He slid in and out of her just like she needed it.

J.R. began to move faster, and Shekira quickened her pace to match his. Suddenly, Shekira pulled off the rubber, got on her knees, and took J.R. into her mouth. She teased his head and then worked her way down his shaft. She slid her lips and tongue up and down his length, and when she felt it getting harder, Shekira relaxed the muscles in her throat and used the roof of her mouth to apply a little pressure on his shaft.

"Damn, Shekira!"

She stopped suddenly. "I'm not ready for you to cum yet." Shekira spat on his dick, stroked it, straddled his body, and lowered herself onto him.

"Fuck me and make me cum," Shekira shouted and slowly began to move her hips back and forth. She bounced up and down on his dick.

J.R. was in ecstasy. He leaned forward and pulled her nipples into his mouth, teasing them as he pounded her. J.R. arched his back and began pushing his dick into her as deep and as hard as he could. The force of his hard, deep thrusts knocked Shekira forward, and she collapsed on his chest, but she kept bringing that wet pussy down as hard and as fast as she could. When his whole body locked, Shekira's head drifted back, her eyes and mouth opened wide, and she screamed just as J.R.'s phone rang.

Chapter Seven

"What did he say?" Barlowe asked when Arya put down the phone.

"He didn't answer."

"Call Nikki."

Arya rolled her eyes, but she picked up the phone and called Nikki. She didn't like Nikki, and she knew the feeling was mutual, so she was hoping to talk to J.R. It had been days since she'd seen him, and being as spoiled as she was, Arya didn't like that. As she dialed Nikki's number, she thought about the first time she had seduced J.R.

She was home alone and horny when a recently-turned-eighteen J.R. came to the house looking for Barlowe. She'd watched him grow into manhood, and now that he was a man, he was wearing it well.

"Pete's not here," she told him that day.

"Well, tell Uncle Pete I came through," J.R. said and was about to leave when Arya stopped him.

"There is something you can do for me before you go."

"What's that?"

"Follow me." Arya led J.R. out of the house to the pool. "There's a box on the shelf in the pool house that I can't reach. Would you get it for me, please?"

"Sure. No problem."

She opened the door, and they went inside.

"Which one?" J.R. asked, looking up at the shelf with his back to her so he didn't see that Arya had locked the door. When he reached up for the box, Arya palmed a handful of dick.

"What are you doing?" he said, quickly dropping his hand to his sides.

"What does it feel like I'm doing?"

"We shouldn't be doing this." He put his hands on her shoulders and pushed her away. "What about Uncle Pete?" J.R. asked, but his dick was rock hard in Arya's hand.

"I'm not going to tell him. Are you?" She reached inside his pants and began to jerk him off. "I know you want me. I've seen how you look at me when you think he's not looking."

J.R. moved his hands away from her shoulders, and Arya brought his head to hers and kissed him gently. She pulled down his zipper.

"This is so wrong," he said, but he relaxed and let it happen. Arya squatted in front of him and started to undo his pants. "We can't do . . . shit!"

J.R.'s words got caught in his throat as Arya took him into her hot, wet mouth. It was a scene in her mind that she often masturbated to.

She made the call to Nikki.

"Hello," a still groggy Nikki answered.

"Hello, Nikki. It's Arya."

"What you want?"

"Pete wants to see you."

"Tell him I'll be there as soon as I can," she said and slammed the phone down on the nightstand.

"What did she say?" Barlowe asked when Arya put down the phone.

"She said she'd be here as soon as possible."

Barlowe nodded.

"I'm gonna try J.R. again," she said and dialed the number. Once again, Arya got no answer. It was unusual for him not to answer Barlowe's call. She hoped that he was all right.

Nikki dragged herself out of bed and headed for the shower, wondering what Barlowe wanted. It had only been a day since her takeover began, so she knew that he couldn't have a problem with what she was doing. Especially since he had backed her play the night before with Wilson. Once she was dressed and ready to leave, she called J.R., but like Arya, she got no answer.

"He's probably knee-deep in some pussy," Nikki said aloud and got in her car.

When she arrived at Barlowe's house, Reggie, his long-time bodyguard, escorted Nikki to the library, where Barlowe was waiting with Arya.

"How's it going, Nikki?" he asked.

"I'm all right. What did you wanna see me about?"

Arya stood up and brought Nikki an image of two men. "Who is this?"

"That's Driton Berisha and Burim Gashi. They're Albanians that I made the mistake of becoming involved with," he said.

He looked at Arya. She was the one who had introduced them, so she felt responsible—because she was. She had met them through one of his old contacts, who told her that they were new in town and their business would net Barlowe a considerable profit from his investment. On the strength of that referral and his trust in Arya, Barlowe fronted them product. The deal was for half a million dollars, of which they paid back a quarter million.

"But that was weeks ago, and they've been radio silent since then. That is, until today. Today, I get a call from Berisha, and he says he got the money and is looking to do business." Barlowe paused. "Fuck that. I ain't doing business with these fucks. Just get me my money."

"Understood. Where's the meet?"

"Arya," Barlowe said, and she got up and handed Nikki a piece of paper. "Warehouse space on Stanley Avenue."

Nikki was about to get up, but she had a question. "Who handled the original deal?"

"J.R.," Arya said quickly.

"I called him, but he didn't answer," Barlowe said.

"He didn't answer when I called him either," Nikki said and stood up.

"You're not worried about him, are you?" Arya asked as Nikki headed for the door.

"Nope. I'm sure he's just getting some pussy, and he'll call me when he gets off it."

Nikki saw the jealous look on Arya's face. *Not her, too. Damn, baby brother*, she thought, shaking her head as she left the library.

"What's up, Nikki?" Cairo asked when he took her call.

"You seen J.R.?"

"Not today. What's up?"

"I need you and Butchie to meet me at a warehouse on Stanley Avenue."

"The Albanians."

"You know about this?"

"Yeah. Me and Butch went with J.R. when he did the deal. Nasty muthafuckas."

"They say they're ready to pay up. You think it's gonna be a problem?"

"I can't say for sure. But they were assholes, so I'd be ready for whatever."

"Got you. How long before you get there?"

"Thirty minutes."

"See you there," Nikki said and ended the call. She made another call to J.R., and once again, she got voicemail. "When you get this message, I need you to meet me at the warehouse on Stanley Avenue where you did that deal with the Albanians."

Thirty minutes later, Cairo and Butch pulled up outside the warehouse and looked around for Nikki's car. She had arrived a while ago and parked across the street. She got out of her car when she saw them, walked to the front door of the warehouse, and waited.

"Ready?" Butch asked.

"Let's go," Nikki said, grabbing the handle to go inside the warehouse.

Once they were inside, they saw Driton Berisha and Burim Gashi standing by a table to make the exchange. Nikki saw the metal briefcase on the table.

"That my money?" Nikki asked, pointing to the case.

"It is. But I notice that you are empty-handed. We had a deal."

"Yeah, well. You *had* a deal until you fucked around and made the man wait on his money."

"Not acceptable."

"I don't give a fuck what you think is not acceptable. That's how it's gonna be. Now, open it," Nikki demanded.

Driton Berisha and Burim Gashi glanced at one another. Cairo looked around and saw more men come out of the shadows.

"Gun!" Cairo shouted just before one started shooting at them.

Driton Berisha and Burim Gashi pulled out their weapons and began firing at Nikki. She ran for cover, took out her gun, and returned their fire. Cairo and Butch took cover and exchanged gunfire with the man.

Nikki began firing as Cairo and Butch made it to cover. She fired and hit one of the shooters with two shots in his chest. Butch fired a couple of shots and hit the second shooter. Nikki saw the briefcase was still on the table, and she thought about making a run to get it. She stood up and fired a couple of shots, but she had to take cover when the last of the shooters began firing at her with an AK.

While he was shooting it out with Nikki, Butch aimed and fired, hitting the man with several shots, and he went down. With their backup shooters down, Berisha and Gashi tried to make a run for it. As Nikki and Cairo fired at Berisha and Gashi, Butch went after the briefcase, thinking it was strange that they'd leave without it. Before they could make it to the exit, they were shot in the back.

When the shooting stopped, Nikki and Cairo came out from cover as Butch opened the case.

"Empty."

"What?" Nikki said and went to look.

"It's empty, Nikki."

"This was a setup from the start."

Chapter Eight

Body Heat was a small strip club with a bar and a small stage. There were better clubs to watch erotic dancers, but Body Heat was where Sky danced, so that was where you'd find Brick every night. And if he wasn't there, he'd be back soon.

Nikki paid to get in and went to the bar. While she waited for the lone bartender, she looked around the club. It was packed with men with money in their hands, and there were women doing table dances, happily taking that cash from them. It made her wonder why her father and Barlowe never opened a strip club.

Maybe I should look into opening one, she thought as the bartender finally got to her.

"What are you drinking?"

"Absolut on the rocks."

Without a word, the bartender spun around and grabbed the bottle of Absolut and a glass. He filled it with ice and then poured her drink.

"Here you go," he said, placing the drink in front of Nikki.

She dropped a fifty on the bar. "Keep the change."

When the bartender reached for the bill, Nikki put her hand on it.

"You seen Brick?"

"He left about ten, fifteen minutes ago." He quickly looked around the tiny club until he was sky-dancing. "But he'll be back."

"Thanks," Nikki said, moving her hand and picking up her drink.

"I'll check back to check on you."

For the next twenty minutes, Nikki sipped her drink. The bartender had just made her another drink and placed it in front of her when he saw Brick enter the club.

"There's your boy," he said to Nikki and pointed.

Nikki watched as Brick made his way through the crowd and sat down at a table close to where Sky was dancing.

"Thanks." Nikki paid her tab and got up from the bar.

Nikki was tall and slim, and the Jacquemus minidress and four-inch stilettos she was wearing that night showed off her legs; therefore, as she weaved through the tables to get to Brick, she attracted the attention of the men.

"What's up, Brick?"

"Nikki! What's poppin'?"

"Mind if I sit?"

"Shit yeah."

Nikki sat down at the table.

"Heard you got the new sheriff," he said.

"Word travels fast."

"Yeah, well, Nikki." He shrugged his shoulders. "You ran off Wilson and killed Paddington." Brick laughed. "That kind of news tends to get around."

"I at least give Wilson a choice."

"You did. Shows you got a good heart. But I was wondering how you being the new sheriff is gonna affect our arrangement."

"For the time being, our arrangement still stands. I will let you know in advance when that changes."

"But things are going to change?"

"Yes. Things are definitely going to change."

When Nikki left Body Heat, she thought about hunting down Dobie. But he might be anywhere, and she was tired, so she drove to her mother's house, took a bath, and went to bed. Before she went to sleep, Nikki sent Dobie a text letting him know that she wanted to see him the following day.

It was after eleven when Nikki woke up. She checked her phone, and Dobie had responded.

I'm in the Bronx. Give me a call when you get up there, and I'll tell you where to meet me.

Nikki got out of bed, and once she took a shower and got dressed, she went downstairs. She found Naomi on the living room couch, watching television.

"Hey, Mommy," Nikki said, sitting on the couch next to her mother.

"Hey, Nikki. Did you sleep well?"

"Yeah. I guess I needed some sleep."

"You hungry?"

"I could eat something."

"There's shrimp salad in the refrigerator."

"I love your shrimp salad." Nikki got up and went into the kitchen. She got some shrimp salad and some crackers and returned to the living room to watch the rest of *The View* with her mother.

After she finished eating, Nikki said goodbye to Naomi and set off for the Bronx. She was on the Cross Bronx Expressway when she made the call to Dobie.

"Sup, Nikki?"

"It's all on you."

"Why don't you meet me at the pizza shop on 225th. If I ain't there when you get there, order me a slice."

"See you when you get there," Nikki said, ending the call and driving to the pizza shop.

When she arrived, Dobie wasn't there, so she stepped to the counter and ordered two slices. Even though she had just eaten, there was no turning down good pizza. Dobie arrived just as the slices were coming out of the oven.

"Sup, Nikki?"

"Just in time to pay for these slices."

"No worries." Dobie paid for the slices and put cheese and red peppers on his. "Let's walk."

"As soon as you hand me the cheese," Nikki said, and once she had hooked up her slice, she followed Dobie out of the pizza shop.

"So, what's up?" Dobie took a bit of his slice.

"There's been some changes."

"So, are you here to kill me?"

"Never that."

"Then what kind of changes are we talking about here?"

"Barlowe handed me power. This is my house now." Nikki took a bite of her slice.

"What happened to Barlowe?"

"He's still the boss." Nikki thought for a second or two. "He's semi-retired."

"Living the good life."

"Like he always has."

"Congratulations."

"I'm here to offer you an opportunity."

"I like opportunity. You have my attention."

"I'm in a position to offer you a better price."

"I'm listening for the catch."

"The catch is that with that better price, you buy more product. You make more money. It's a win-win for both of us."

"I'm in." Dobie took a bite of his slice. "This is right on time."

"How so?"

"That's what I'm doing up here. I'm expanding, and the better price will go a long way toward making that happen."

Nikki stopped at her car. "Like I said, it's a win-win for both of us."

"I see this." Dobie thought about the possibilities. "Yeah, this will work well for both of us, Nikki."

She unlocked her door. "I'll be in touch soon." She got in the car.

"Where you on your way to?"

"I'm on my way to talk to Jackson."

"Mind if I tag along?"

"Get in."

"It'll give us a chance to talk," Dobie said, but he had reasons of his own for wanting to see Jackson. He looked over at Nikki as she drove and knew that she wouldn't be happy about what he planned to do.

"Where you at?" Nikki asked Jackson when he answered the phone.

Jackson hesitated. "I'm out on the island. What up?"

"We need to talk about something. Text me your address."

"Hold on." Jackson sent the text.

"Got it. I'm on my way," Nikki said, ending the call. "He's out on the island."

Dobie made himself comfortable. "Glad you're driving."

"Right," Nikki said, programming the address into the navigation system.

Traffic was light, so a little over an hour later, Nikki and Dobie arrived in Dix Hills at the address Jackson gave them. Nikki and Dobie got out of the car and approached the house. While Dobie stood back, Nikki rang the bell. It was a while before the door opened.

"What's up, Nikki?" Jackson said and walked away from the door.

"What's up?"

Nikki stepped inside with Dobie, and he closed the door. Jackson turned around and saw Dobie.

"Oh, shit!"

He turned to run for his gun. Dobie took out his gun and shot Jackson in the back before he could get to it. Nikki took out her gun and pointed it at Dobie.

"What the fuck, Dobie?"

Dobie put up his hands. "Sorry, Nikki."

Nikki looked at Jackson's body, lying face down with a pool of blood forming around him.

"Damn."

"I'm sorry, Nikki. Give me a chance to explain." Dobie paused. "I'm gonna put the gun down."

Nikki nodded.

Dobie leaned forward and slowly put the gun on the floor in front of him and put his hands up. Nikki motioned with her gun, and Dobie took a step back. Nikki lowered her gun but didn't put it away.

"You can put your hands down."

Dobie lowered his hands. "Thank you."

"Let's hear it."

"You know Jackson always had a nose for the product, right?"

"Yeah, I heard that." But as long as it didn't interfere with the money, Nikki was good with it.

"He started smoking."

"I didn't know that."

"When his boy Chuck stepped to him about it, Jackson stole a lot of the product and money and disappeared. They've been looking for him ever since."

"How long has he been ghost?"

"I don't know."

"How'd you get involved with this?"

"Me and Chuck been cool a long time. He reached out to me, explained the situation and asked for my help in covering their loss so you wouldn't find out. They had this idea that you and J.R. would kill them all over Uncle Pete's money."

"They had that part right."

"I told them I'd help them cover their loss, but they work for me now. They agreed, so I had a vested interest in finding our friend there."

Nikki took out her phone, went through her contacts, and dialed a number. "Chuck Baby. What's up?"

"What's poppin', Nikki?"

"I need to talk to Jackson, but he ain't answering my calls. You seen him?"

Chuck paused before answering. "Honestly, Nikki, I don't know where the muthafucka is."

"What's up with that?"

"Jackson started smoking the product, and when he tried to do a little intervention, this nigga steals a lot of product and money, and nobody has seen him since."

"How long was this?"

"Two weeks."

"How come I'm just now hearing about this?"

"I wasn't ready to die for this nigga's sins, so I reached out to Dobie and made a deal. I was gonna tell you about it once we got right."

"Thanks, Chuck Baby. You just saved Dobie's life," she said, ending the call and lowering her weapon.

"Okay, what now?"

"I'm gonna have a look around and see if there's any left."

"Go ahead."

Chapter Nine

Francine grabbed J.R.'s dick, sucked it a few times, and then lowered herself and once again took his dick into the wetness between her thighs. She rode him slowly, and he licked and sucked her nipples as her legs began trembling, and he pushed it harder into her. Francine bore down on him and increased her pace. He could feel that she was about to cum again, so he grabbed her by the shoulders and plunged as deeply as he could into her warmth.

Francine got excited and began twisting her hips as J.R. ran his hands over her thighs and her ass. She rubbed her hands over her breasts and squeezed her nipples. Then he flipped Francine over on her back. She spread her legs, and he dove into that wet pussy as if it were the greatest thing that he had ever experienced—because it was.

Francine started rocking her hips into him while she rubbed and squeezed her breasts again. J.R. pulled her to his chest. Their bodies moved in sync with each other's rhythm.

"Cum hard for me," she demanded. "I want to feel you explode inside me."

J.R. held her tighter, and Francine milked his dick with her pussy as hard as she could. He matched her stroke for stroke, until he felt himself begin to expand inside her. He fucked her harder, moving in and out of her faster and harder until they both exploded, and they collapsed in each other's arms.

"You shouldn't fuck me like that," Francine said as soon as she caught her breath. "You ain't ever gonna get rid of me if you keep fuckin' me like that."

"Who said I ever wanna get rid of you? J.R. asked as Francine got out of bed.

"Nobody."

"Remy can't handle you, so you come to a man that can."

Francine picked up the white Nili Lotan Rolland wide-leg jeans, black Paige cropped bouclé jacket, and Mariela cotton crew neck T-shirt from the floor, where she had tossed them in the heat of passion, then headed toward the shower.

While she showered and got dressed, J.R. thought about Nikki and her plan. He was a little disappointed to know that she had all this planned and felt like she needed to keep him in the dark, but he understood. J.R. also understood the reason why she felt that way. He was and always had been overly loyal to the man he called Uncle Pete, in spite of what his mother and Nikki said to him about where his loyalty should lie.

"You need to be loyal to your sister. Not that nigga," Naomi had told him so many times over the years. But things were different now, or at least they were going to be different. He did feel good that she had trusted him with her plan and no longer felt the need to keep him at arm's length.

When Francine came out of the bathroom dressed and ready to go, J.R. got out of bed so he could walk her to the door.

"Where you on your way to now?"

Francine glanced at her watch. "I gotta meet Remy."

"You want me to drive you?" J.R. joked.

"Wouldn't that be something? But no, I'm meeting him at one of his stash houses, and he probably would not want me to bring you along with me. But you never know."

"Probably not." J.R. wrapped his arms around her waist and kissed her neck. "But you would tell me if I asked you where his stash house is, right?"

"Of course I would. There are no secrets between you and me."

"Well, where is it?"

Francine stopped and removed his hands from around her waist. "You serious?"

"Yeah, I'm serious. Where's his spot?"

Francine looked at J.R. for a while, and then she shook her head. "I am so weak for you. You know that?"

"Yeah, I know."

Francine stepped to J.R.'s chest and got on her toes. She put her arms around his neck. "Don't you ever stop fuckin' me." She kissed him. "Never."

"Never."

"He's got a house on Sagamore Road. That's where the stash house is."

Francine kissed him again, and then she left the house to meet Remy at his stash house. J.R. stood at the door and waited for her to get into the Porsche GT4 that Remy had paid for before he went back into the house. He sat down on the couch and called Nikki.

"Where you at?" he asked.

"I'm at mom's house. Why?"

"Stay there. I got something to tell you about."

"I'll be here," Nikki said and ended the call with her brother, wondering what he wanted to tell her.

"And she just up and told you?" Nikki asked.

"Yup."

"Damn. Is the dick that good to her?"

"And I quote: don't ever stop fuckin' me."

"Okay. We check it out tonight, and if she's right, we hit the spot the next night. One more thing. Jackson is dead."

"What happened? He didn't wanna go along with the new program?" he asked.

"No. He stole the product and money."

"He had to die."

"Guess that's why he's dead."

That night, she and J.R. were on Sagamore Road, checking out the house.

"I'm gonna walk around the house," J.R. said. "See if I can get a look inside without being seen."

Nikki handed him a pair of binoculars. "Be careful, and don't get too close. You hear me?"

"Yeah, Nikki, I hear you," he said and got out of the car.

J.R. walked around the house, and then he went around to the back at what he thought was a safe distance. He raised the binoculars and tried to get a look inside the house.

"What did you see?" Nikki asked when he got back in the car with her.

"I saw two men in the living room. Ain't much furniture and shit in there, but in one of the bedrooms, there's a chest freezer, and there are two metal cabinets with doors and a lock. They got a chain with a padlock around the lock."

"I think it's safe to say that's where they keeping the dope. You recognize the niggas in the house?"

"One of them. His name is Rob."

"How you know him?"

"He used to be security at XL for years."

"I guess this is a promotion. Let's go."

J.R. started the car and drove off. "So, what you think?"

"Get Cairo and Butchie. We gonna hit the spot tomorrow night."

That next night, Nikki parked in front of the house on Sagamore Road.

"Sup, Rob?" Cairo said. Butch and J.R. were standing on either side of the door.

"What are you doing here?" Rob asked.

Cairo, Butch, and J.R. all raised their silencer-equipped weapons. "Killing you," Cairo said and shot Rob in the head.

They rushed into the house. There were two other men in the living room. They were armed with AKs. As they were reaching for their guns, Butch and J.R. shot them. Cairo shot Rob twice more in the chest before he came into the house. Butch and J.R. did the same with the two men with the AKs, and then the three headed toward the back of the house where J.R. said they kept the dope. The door was padlocked, so Butch shot the lock off, and they went inside. The only things in the room were a chest freezer and two metal cabinets. They were padlocked as well. J.R. shot the locks off, and he opened the freezer, which was filled with kilos of cocaine. They emptied the freezer, closed the door, and then they went to the cabinets. Butch opened the doors and found it filled with cash. They quickly emptied the cabinets.

Once they were done, they left the house and walked casually to the car. Nikki saw them coming and got out. She walked around to the trunk and had it open when they got there. She took out the two gas cans that she had brought along with her.

"Burn it."

"What?" Butch asked, and she handed him a gas can.

"Go back in there, pour gas on the dead guys, and then set the place on fire."

"On it." Cairo smiled and took the other can from Nikki as J.R. put the stolen dope in the trunk.

"Be right back," Cairo said, and he went back to the house with Butch.

As Nikki had instructed, Cairo and Butch poured gas on the dead men before emptying the cans around the house. Once that was done, they came out on the porch, and Cairo dropped a match on the gasoline trail that he had left. The house caught on fire quickly. They waited and watched until the tiny house was totally engulfed in flames before Nikki told Butch to drive them away from the burning structure.

Chapter Ten

When Nikki came out of the warehouse with Butch and Cairo, J.R. pulled up and hopped out of his car.

"What's goin' on?" he asked as they came toward him.

Nikki kept walking to her car. "We came here to collect from the Albanians, but they beat us."

J.R. walked alongside Nikki to her car. "Are they dead?"

"Yeah." She got in. "Meet me at Barlowe's."

When they got to Barlowe's house, he was waiting there with Arya. While Cairo and Butch waited, Nikki and J.R. went to tell Barlowe what happened. Nikki watched Arya's face light up when J.R. came into the library.

"You get my money?" Barlowe asked as soon as they walked in.

"No," Nikki said.

"What happened?"

"They did *not* have money. It was a setup," Nikki said, and Barlowe glared angrily at Arya. "Their plan was to rob us. They're dead."

"I'm sorry," Arya said quickly.

"You ought to be sorry. It was you that brought these fucks to me, and now I'm out a quarter mil."

"I'm sorry."

"Get out," Barlowe said quietly, but nobody moved. "I said get the fuck outta here!" he screamed at the top of his lungs. Slowly, Nikki, J.R., and Arya got up and left the library.

"You gonna be all right?" J.R. asked Arya when they were in the hallway.

"I'll be all right. He'll calm down after a while," she said as they got to the living room where Cairo and Butch were waiting. They stood up.

"Come on, let's go," she said, and they followed her to the door.

"Where are y'all going?" Arya asked.

"Outta here," Nikki said, and they left the house. Arya followed them outside.

"Can I talk to you for a second, J.R.?" Arya asked when they made it to their cars.

"Just a second," J.R. said and walked up to Nikki. "Where you on your way to?"

"XL to see if Rashard got my money."

"I'll meet you there," J.R. said and walked back to where Arya was waiting.

When Nikki, Cairo, and Butch arrived at Club XL, it was still early in the evening. Happy hour was just getting started, and the crowd was just beginning to file in. Nikki approached one of the servers.

"Rashard here?"

"No. I haven't seen him today. But there's a letter addressed to you on the desk in his office."

"Thanks," Nikki said, and she went to the office.

As promised, there was a letter on the desk addressed to Nikki. She sat down at the desk and opened it. It read:

> *Nikki,*
> *Your money is in the safe.*
> *The combination is 86-40-12.*
> *I'm out. Please, don't try to find me, and let me live.*
> *Rashard*

"Ain't that a bitch." Nikki started laughing, and then she read the letter to Cairo and Butch. They laughed, too. She handed Butch the letter.

"Check it out," Nikki said, and Butch went to the safe.

"There's money in here."

"Count it."

Once Butch counted the money and saw it was all there, he and Cairo left Nikki alone in the office. When they went out into the club, Rah-Rah was there with Shekira. She had spent the day at Thatcher's studio, meeting the other dancers and learning the routine.

As soon as Shekira saw J.R. come into Club XL and head for the office, she got up from the bar and left to follow him.

"What's up, Rah-Rah?" Cairo asked.

"I'm good. I'm good. Listen, let me holla at you for a second," she said, and Cairo stepped a little closer to her.

"What's up?"

"You got anything on you?"

"What are we talking about here, Rah-Rah?"

"You know." She leaned closer. "Some blow."

Cairo looked surprised because he didn't know that she was into that. But he thought Rah-Rah was fine, and he had always wanted to fuck her, so it was on.

"Powder or rock?"

"Rock."

"How much you want?"

"Fifty."

Cairo gazed at the way Rah-Rah's breasts looked in the As It May Koresma color-blocked bowtie minidress that she was wearing. He dug in his pocket, leaned close to Rah-Rah, and kissed her on the cheek.

"That's for you." He handed her the package. "Come see me when you want some more."

"I will," Rah-Rah said, smiling, and walked away quickly.

Butch joined Cairo at the bar. "What Rah-Rah fine ass want?" he asked.

"Some rocks."

"I didn't know she smoked."

"Neither did I, but she'll be back for more."

"No doubt," Butch said.

On their way out of the club, Cairo saw Shekira talking to Rah-Rah before Rah-Rah rushed toward the exit. When J.R. came out to the office with Nikki, he saw Shekira sitting there, and then he saw Cairo and Butch leaving and rushed to catch up with them.

"Let's go," he said, and they fell in behind him.

"Hey, J.R.," Shekira said when he was close enough.

"Hey." J.R. stopped. Cairo and Butch kept walking.

"What's your rush?"

"I need to catch up with my boys."

"Where y'all going?"

"We got business to take care of."

They didn't really have business to take care of. J.R. just didn't feel like being bothered with Shekira, no matter how good that pussy was.

Not now, anyway.

"I'll call you when we're done." He started and put his arms around her. "Maybe we can get together later and pick up where we left off this morning."

"I'll be waiting for your call," Shekira said, and she watched as J.R. caught up with Cairo and Butch, and they left the club.

Nikki looked around the club until she saw the people she was looking for. Once she saw them, she went to the table where they were sitting.

"Evening, ladies," she said to her three friends, Sierra, Megan, and Chrystal. The four had grown up together and had been friends since their school days. With Nikki as a best friend, the three were in the clubs that she now ran every night.

"What's up, Nikki?" Megan said.

She and Nikki were unlikely best friends, Megan being white and Nikki being Black. They met while they were in elementary school and quickly became the best of friends. Sierra joined the crew when they were in the seventh grade, and Chrystal began hanging out with them when they got to high school. The four of them couldn't be more different. Nikki was well on her way to being the gangster Pete Barlowe was grooming her to be. Megan was the cool one. No matter what was going on—and they got into a lot—Megan seemed unphased.

One night, she was out with Nikki, and a woman shoved a gun in her face. "Leave my man alone, bitch!" the woman shouted with a crazed look in her eyes.

Megan took two steps forward so the barrel of the crazed woman's gun was pressed against her forehead. The woman's hand started trembling.

"You can shoot me now. 'Cause I'm not gonna stop fuckin' him. His dick and head games are too strong," Megan said and snatched the gun from her shaking hand.

Chrystal was the wild, down-for-whatever one. When Megan took the gun, Chrystal pulled the woman from the back, and she stumbled to the floor. With the house free of civilians, Chrystal started kicking her.

"Free for all!" she shouted, and Megan and Sierra joined in. Sierra was the prissy one, until you made her mad, and then she was ready to fight.

"Let me get these earrings off," Sierra said as she took off her shoes. "Then I'm gonna beat your skinny bitch ass," she said and busted the girl's nose with the first punch. There wasn't much fight left in the skinny bitch after that.

They were four pretty girls, and the Big Apple was their playground.

"Let's talk in the office," Nikki said, and they all got up and followed Nikki to the office.

"What's going on?" Chrystal asked when they got to the office and sat down.

Nikki stood before them. "I need your VIP passes."

"Why?" Sierra asked as she was going in her purse to get it.

"Never mind that. I need your passes, please," Nikki said with her hand out.

Each of them got their VIP passes from their purses and handed them to Nikki.

"Thank you," she said with a big grin on her face and tossed the VIP passes into the garbage. Sierra, Megan, and Chrystal's mouths dropped open.

"What you do that for?" a wide-eyed Megan asked.

"What does it look like? I'm revoking your VIP status," Nikki said, barely able to contain her laughter at the sight of their faces.

"Did we do something wrong?" Chrystal asked. She was at one of the clubs every night. Chrystal loved the atmosphere, the people, and the music. Not having her VIP status felt like a punishment.

"No. I was going to make a speech, but I changed my mind."

"What's up?" Sierra asked.

"We've known each other for a long time. Y'all are my best friends, and I love you."

"And that's why you're revoking our passes," Chrystal quipped.

"I'm sure she has her reasons, Chrystal," Megan said sadly.

"I do. Long story short, there's been some changes. So, as of right now, you're the new manager here, Sierra."

"What happened to D'marco and Rashard?"

"They're out."

"Thank you, Nikki."

"Chrystal, you think you can handle Marquee?"

"Hell yeah. You know that's my spot."

"I know."

"Thank you, Nikki."

"And you, Megan, the salt to my pepper."

"The skinny girls," Megan said and laughed.

"The stick figures," Nikki said, recalling one of their many nicknames.

"I haven't heard that one in years," Megan said.

"You two were skinny," Sierra said.

"But look at them now," Chrystal commented.

"Anyway. Megan, the Palace is yours."

"Thank you, Nikki."

"Y'all think you can handle it?"

"Shit, yeah," Chrystal said. "You know I've been wanting to run a club for a long time."

"Now's your chance."

"What exactly are we doing?"

"Your title is general manager, but your job is to watch my back. You make sure that everything needed to run the club is done and we are ready to open. All of the managers report to you. Learn from them, know their jobs, so you can do them if it becomes necessary." Nikki stood up. "Come on, Sierra. I'll introduce you to your staff and get started with your training. Then we'll go to Marquee and the Palace." She laughed. "You party girls got jobs now. Don't disappoint me."

"We won't," Sierra said.

After Nikki got Sierra started, she left Club XL with Megan and Chrystal, and they went to their new clubs.

Once she got them situated, Nikki didn't feel like driving home, so she checked into Arlo SoHo on Hudson Street. Her intention was to pamper herself with her favorite relaxing phyto-aromatic body ritual and a stone-soother massage.

Chapter Eleven

When J.R. woke up the next afternoon, he had to shield his eyes from the bright sun shining through the window. He had to look around and think about where he was. He looked in the bed next to him and saw Shekira. He was in her apartment, having come there after he finished the job with Cairo and Butch. He sat on the edge of the bed and looked over his shoulder at Shekira.

"Damn, that's some good pussy," he said aloud and stood up.

J.R. gathered his clothes and went to the bathroom to shower. While the hot water beat down on his neck and back, he thought about the night before, when he had caught up with Cairo and Butch after leaving Shekira at Club XL.

"What y'all getting ready to do?" J.R. asked.

"About to make some money," Butch said.

"You want in?" Cairo asked.

"Hell yeah. What's the deal?"

"Get in the car, and we'll tell you all about it on the way," Butch said, and the three got in Cairo's car.

When they got to the building, the three men watched the door as a man took up a position outside the foyer.

"That's the sentry," Cairo said.

"Move into position," Butch said.

"You know what to do?" Cairo asked J.R.

"I got it. Let's do it."

J.R. and Cairo got out of the car, which Butch had parked down the street. Cairo immediately started walking toward the building. Once he had reached a certain point, J.R. began walking behind him. Butch got out of the car and started toward the building.

When Cairo approached the building, he stopped and looked around like he was lost. The sentry came out to meet him.

"You need to keep moving," the sentry said.

Now that he had stepped forward, J.R. stepped up behind him and put a gun to his head.

"Inside."

When they stepped inside, Butch was in a position outside the building. Cairo hit the sentry with two shots, one to the head and the other to his chest. J.R. and Cairo dragged the sentry out of sight. Once that was done, the three went upstairs, putting on ski masks in the hallway, and moved into position outside the door.

Cairo kicked in the door, and J.R. and Butch rushed in. J.R. hit one man with two to the chest as he was reaching for his gun. The second man got to his gun, but Butch caught him in the chest before he could get a shot off. The third man jumped up from his chair and tried to make it to his gun on the dining room table. Before he got very far, Cairo entered the apartment and shot him in the back of the head.

One man was trying to gather up the drugs from the table. He grabbed his gun and fired at J.R., who returned fire and hit him with two shots in his chest. Another man stepped out of a back room and shot at Butch, then ducked back into the room for cover. Butch shot back blindly at the man as he ran. The man came out of the room, firing shots in all directions, and made a run for the door. J.R. hit him in the back before he could make it out the door.

J.R. looked around and saw Cairo shooting it out with one man. J.R. fired at him and took cover to reload as the man went down. Suddenly, there was quiet in the apartment. J.R., Cairo, and Butch looked at one another.

"Wasn't expecting all that," Butch said.

"It was just supposed to be two guys," Cairo said.

"Fuck all that now. Let's get what we came for and get outta here," J.R. said, and after a quick search of the apartment, they found the money and the cocaine, and the three left the apartment.

J.R. turned off the water and got out of the shower. Once he was dressed, he came out of the bathroom. Shekira was still in bed sleeping.

"Damn, that's some good pussy," he repeated aloud, because it was, and then left her room and her apartment as quietly as possible.

J.R. was in his car driving home when he got a call from Nikki. "What's up, sis?"

"I'm good. What's up with you today?"

"Nothing much. Why? What's up?"

"I just wanted to remind you that we're having dinner with Mommy tonight."

"I forgot all about that. Thanks, Nikki."

"I figured you did." Nikki laughed. "You always do."

"Call it a character flaw."

"Braindead by Uncle Pete was more what I was thinking," Nikki mused. "See you there. At five!" Nikki shouted before she ended the call. "Try not to be late."

It was just before five that afternoon when J.R. arrived at the house on Wood Valley Lane that his father had built and Barlowe had paid for after his death. It was the house where he and Nikki grew up. It was also the place where their father was murdered.

When J.R. went into the house, he could hear Eyewitness News playing on the television as he passed the living room on his way to the kitchen.

"There's my baby boy," Naomi said when he came into the kitchen.

"Hey, Ma," J.R. said and hugged his mother. "What's up, Nikki?" She was sitting at the table in the kitchen.

"What's up?"

"Let me holla at you for a second," J.R. said and turned to leave the kitchen.

"Dinner is almost ready, so don't go too far," Naomi requested and returned her attention to the meal she was preparing.

"Yes, Mommy," Nikki said, following her brother out of the kitchen and into the living room. "What's up?"

"That's for you." J.R. handed Nikki an envelope. "We did a little thing last night."

"Thank you," Nikki said, peeking into the envelope and seeing the cash.

A news reporter's voice came from the television. "The police department is investigating the suspected gang-land murders of seven men at the Red Hook Houses. The murders appear to be drug-related," the news reporter said. "Anyone with any information is encouraged to contact the police department."

Nikki looked at her brother. "That for you?" she asked, and J.R. nodded his acknowledgment. "Whose spot was it?"

"It was one of Garraway's spots."

Duncan Garraway was an organized crime syndicate figure who controlled a significant part of the heroin, cocaine, and marijuana trade. He was the competition. Back in the day, Garraway, in partnership with Fast Eddie Marx and Pistol Pete Barlowe, had formed the Council, where disputes among the criminals were settled and distribution problems and other drug trade–related issues were handled. The Council was abruptly dissolved when Eddie Marx was murdered. Since then, Barlowe and Garraway had become bitter enemies, and a state of war, a cold war, existed between the two organizations.

"Are you sure that was a good idea? I'm in no mood to go to war with those fucks."

"I didn't know it was one of Garraway's spots until we got there, but not to worry. There are seven dead for a reason."

"Dead men don't point fingers," Nikki said, hoping there would be no repercussions.

"Dinner is ready!" Naomi called to her children from the kitchen.

Nikki and J.R. left the living room and went into the kitchen, where their mother had dinner ready and on the table. The three sat down to a meal of slow-cooked pork ribs that fell off the bone, baked sweet potatoes with cinnamon, corn, baked mac and cheese, and cornbread. Noami, Nikki, and J.R. held hands.

"Bless us, O God," Noami began. "Bless our food and our drink. Since you redeemed us so dearly and delivered us from evil, as you gave us a share in this food, so may you give us a share in eternal life."

"Amen," Nikki and J.R. said.

J.R. grabbed the platter with the ribs and helped himself before passing it to his sister.

"Should you pass me the mac and cheese, J.R.?" Noami requested.

"Here you go, Mommy."

"Thank you," Naomi said as she helped herself to mac and cheese. "So, what's going on with you?"

"I'm all right, Ma."

"How's sneaky Pete?"

"Uncle Pete is doing fine. He said to say hello. And if there's anything that you need, he said to call him."

"Which I never have, and I never will. I've gone all these years without needing to call him, and I won't start now." Naomi helped herself to sweet potatoes. "You two are much too dependent on that man. Waiting for him to give you what you know is yours."

"Nikki ain't waiting no more," J.R. said without looking up from his food.

"What you talking about?"

"I took over and put people in place at the Palace, Vee's, Marquee, and XL."

"What about the dope and the women?" Naomi wanted to know.

"She's been skimming from drug heads for months," J.R. informed her.

"And we're going to see Amanda Reese, Darvin Westcock, and Steve Stewart tonight."

"You be careful of Silky Stewart. That is one of the most ignorant men I've ever met, and that makes him dangerous."

"Don't worry, Mommy," Nikki said. "I can handle Stewart."

"If not. I'll handle Silky," J.R. said and kept eating.

"Good. It is long past time for you two to take what is rightfully yours. I didn't think Pete's greedy ass would ever do what's right."

"He didn't. I made this happen."

"How?"

"I went to him and said since he was going to hold me and J.R. responsible for shit when it went wrong, he needed to let us run it our way."

"And he went along with that?"

"Yes, ma'am, he did."

"I'm surprised."

The three ate in silence for a while, until Naomi said, "None of that means that you can trust him."

"You don't have to worry about that happening, Mommy. Everybody that I trust is sitting at this table," Nikki said, and she helped herself to more ribs.

Chapter Twelve

Moxy NYC East Village, The Standard, High Line, Conrad New York Downtown, Arlo Soho, Hotel 50 Bowery, and Ace Hotel New York were just a few of the hotels that lined the New York skyline, and Barlowe had women working the trade in all of them. They were run by Amanda Reese, Darvin Westcock, and Steve Stewart. Reese and Westcock were young businesspeople who managed the women, unlike Stewart. He was a pimp and had been working for Barlowe for years since the days when Fast Eddie was still alive. Like many of Barlowe's people who had been around a while, Silky, as he was called back in the day, didn't like Nikki and J.R. He thought they were arrogant and disrespectful of him and his position.

Amanda Reese ran the women at Arlo Soho, Hotel 50 Bowery, and the Conrad New York Downtown. She preferred the Conrad, so that was where she conducted business. When Nikki and J.R. walked into the Loopy Doopy rooftop bar, which was located on the 16th floor with Butch and Cairo, Amanda saw them and signaled for them to join her. She had started out walking the streets and working the hotel bars over twenty years ago. As the years passed and things changed, Amanda, who was getting older, made the transition from being the product to the one who packaged and presented the product for sale.

Amanda had heard what was going on, and as far as she was concerned, it didn't affect her or how she chose to run her business. To Amanda, Nikki and J.R. taking over just meant that she handed her fat envelope to someone else.

"Nikki, J.R., how's it going?"

"Going good, Amanda. How about you?" Nikki asked.

"I have no complaints. Everything in my world is fabulous."

"I'm guessing you already know what's going on?" J.R. asked.

"I do," Amanda said, and as discreetly as she could, she passed Nikki an envelope. "Is it appropriate for me to say congratulations?"

Nikki smiled. "It is."

Amanda raised a glass. "Well, congratulations. This has been a long time coming."

"It has."

"You remember when we first met, Nikki? You were so angry with the world." Amanda laughed. "You've come a long way."

"Thank you, Amanda," Nikki said and stood up. "If you need anything, you know how to get in touch with me."

Their next stop was The Moxy NYC East Village, where they talked to Darvin Westcock. Westie, as he was known, ran the women who worked at The Moxy, and The Standard, High Line. Magic Hour Rooftop Bar and Lounge featured an urban amusement park, DJs, and epic skyline views. Westie liked to hang out, and he conducted his business there. Like Amanda, Westie had been a part of the organization for years. He had started out as a driver and then security for a few of the women over the years before he made the transition to management. He, too, had heard about Nikki taking power and was ready with an envelope.

"Thanks, Westie. If you need anything, you know how to get in touch with me," Nikki said. She was about to stand up.

"You going to the Hotel 50 to talk to Stewart now?" Westie asked.

"Yeah, why?"

"Be careful. He's talking about killing you over this foolishness," Westie warned.

"You're kidding me," J.R. said.

"I wish I were. I believe 'over my dead body' were his exact words."

J.R. stood up. "We can do it any way he wants." He chuckled. "Dead is fine with me."

"Thanks for the heads up, Westie. I'm ready for whatever bullshit Silky Stew got. Ain't that right, Butchie?" Nikki asked.

"Sure, you're right. The dumb shit express stops here," Butch said, putting his fingers to his head like a gun and firing.

"Just don't wanna see you walk into something unnecessarily," Westie said.

"Thanks, Westie," Nikki said, and she left the Magic Hour on her way to the Hotel 50 to talk to Steve "Silky" Stewart.

Unlike Barlow and Marx, he was a pimp. The women he pimped worked at Hotel 50 and the Ace Hotel New York. While Eddie and Pete were slinging dope, Silky was running women slinging pussy. The three men had completely different personalities. Where Eddie was quiet and calculating, Silky was loud, flashy, and flamboyant. Pete's personality was somewhere in the middle, and although they got on Eddie's nerves sometimes, the three became the very best of friends.

When Nikki, J.R., Cairo, and Butch arrived at Hotel 50, some of Stewart's thugs saw them and alerted him to their presence in the hotel. Therefore, when they got to the Crown, Stewart and his people were waiting and ready for them.

"Nikki!" Stewart shouted like he was glad to see her.

"What's up, Stew?"

"Same as yesterday." He looked around the lounge at all the women working for him that night. "Getting all of the money that my hoes make for me. Ain't that what you wanted to hear?"

Nikki sat down and signaled for a waitress. "Yeah. You making me money is exactly what I wanna hear and what I came to talk to you about."

"I hear." Stewart laughed as the server arrived.

"What can I get you?"

"Sin Cyn," Nikki said and looked at the men. "What y'all drinking?"

"Johnny Blue on the rocks," J.R. said and sat beside Nikki.

"Lagavulin Distiller's Edition Islay," Butch said, and J.R. laughed.

"What fuck is that?"

"It's a single malt scotch whiskey."

"Whatever," J.R. said, and it was clear to Nikki that Stewart was getting annoyed.

She smiled. "What about you, Cairo?"

"Bacardi Ocho, neat."

"I'll have those out in a minute," the server said and left the table.

"You finished?" Stewart asked.

"Ordering drinks? Yeah, I'm done with that." Nikki laughed. "Waitress is gone, so yeah, definitely done with that."

"So, what you wanna talk to me about, Nikki?"

"You said you already know why I'm here."

"All the same, why don't you stop fuckin' around and tell me?"

"Fuckin' around? Is that what you think I'm doing?"

"Fuck you want, Nikki?"

"I came here to tell you that you're done. At least you're done working for me."

Stewart laughed. "That's funny since I never have worked for you. And if you thought you were gonna waltz into my house and push me out, you were mistaken."

"I don't have to push you out. See, what you don't know is the reason you're done."

Stewart laughed to hide his confusion. "What's that?"

"You ain't got no women," Nikki said, and she held up her hand in the air.

When she snapped her fingers, the women who were working the bar stopped what they were doing and left The Crown.

Stewart stood up quietly. "Where the fuck y'all going?" he shouted to the women as they walked out. "Get your asses back here!" But the women kept walking. The other guests in the bar were looking at them.

"Sit down, Stew. You're embarrassing me and yourself," Nikki said as Stewart watched the last woman walk out of the lounge.

It was then that the server returned with their drinks. While the server placed the drinks on the table and handed drinks to Cairo and Butch, Stewart stood, exchanging angry looks at Nikki.

"Will there be anything else?" the server asked.

"No." Nikki pulled out a wad of bills. She paid the tab and added a generous tip. "I'll let you know if we need anything else."

"Thank you," the server said and left the table.

Stewart waited until the server was far enough away before he leaned forward and pointed in Nikki's face. "It ain't going down like this, Nikki!" he shouted, and his men gathered around him.

Nikki and J.R. stood up. "You wanna do this right here, right now?"

Stewart looked at the crowded lounge. The Crown was his stop. He'd been doing his business there for years, and when this foolishness was over and this little girl was put in her place, he planned to continue doing his business there, so he backed down.

"Another time."

"Another place," Nikki said and shot her drink.

Once J.R., Cairo, and Butch finished their drinks, Nikki got in Stewart's face. "That's a promise," she said and led her men out of The Crown.

"That bitch got a lot of fuckin' nerve coming up in here thinking she could run the boo on me." Stewart laughed. "She got it all wrong." He looked at his men. "Kill that bitch," he said quietly and sat down.

It was just before two o'clock in the morning, and The Crown was getting ready to close. Stewart had hung around to see if the woman Nikki had run off would come back. When they didn't, he checked the hotel and found that none of his so-called women were still in the hotel. He was about to get out of there and go to the Ace Hotel to see if any of his women were still working.

It was early in the morning, so not many people were on the street. Stewart had just stepped outside the hotel on his way to the parking lot to get his car for the ride to the Ace Hotel when a car pulled up in front of him. When J.R. stuck his gun out of the window, the people nearby ran for cover.

"Time to die," he said, and he shot Stewart five times in the chest.

When Stewart went down, the few people on the street who may have witnessed the shooting ran in the opposite direction. J.R. boldly got out of the car and stood over him. He shot Stewart in the head.

"Promise kept."

Chapter Thirteen

Nikki didn't feel like going home again that night, so she drove to her mother's house, went to her old room, and went to sleep. In the morning, she was awakened by the smell of bacon cooking in the kitchen.

"Good morning, Mommy."

A startled Naomi spun around. "You scared me. I didn't know you were here."

"Surprise!" Nikki said and helped herself to coffee.

"Well, good morning. I'll put on some more bacon." Naomi stopped. "You are gonna have breakfast with me, aren't you?"

"Yes, Mommy." Nikki sat down at the table. "If you make your amazing meat lovers baked omelet, and in addition to the sausage, ham, and bacon, I would absolutely love it if you added spinach. You know how much I love spinach."

"Since you were a little girl. It was the only vegetable I could get you to eat then."

Instead of putting on more bacon, Naomi got sausage, ham, and spinach from the refrigerator and started on breakfast.

"Everything all right?" she asked Nikki.

"Yeah, Mommy, everything's fine. I just got a lot on my mind. With the takeover and all."

"How's that going?"

"We took care of Stewart last night."

"I knew you'd have to."

"So did I."

That was why Nikki had talked to Waneesa Pruit. Like Amanda Reese, she had been working the trade since she was seventeen. Now, at age thirty, Waneesa still had her body, but she also had influence over other women who worked for Stewart. Nikki knew that she was going to have to kill Stewart, so she had made a deal with her.

"You do this for me, and his spot is yours."

"What do you want me to do?"

Waneesa had arranged for them to walk out on command.

"I'm surprised that Sneaky Pete was good with you taking over."

"So was I. It got me thinking that maybe I've been wrong about him. Maybe he always intended to hand it all over to us."

"You mean maybe I was wrong about him." Naomi sat down at the table with Nikki. "I'm the reason you don't trust him. I dumped all my distrust and hatred on you. Maybe it wasn't fair to him, but I could only tell you how I felt."

"I'm not blaming you, Mommy. I have no idea what happened between you and him to make you feel that way, and it's not my concern." Nikki paused. "Unless you wanna tell me."

"It wouldn't be my first choice, no."

But Naomi wondered if now was the time to tell Nikki the truth. They weren't kids anymore, and they could take care of themselves. She could tell them the truth and allow them to make their own decisions. The truth had cost her once before, so Naomi was reluctant to say it.

"And I'm not asking you to explain yourself. I just know I need to give him a chance to prove us both wrong."

"Maybe you're right, Nikki." Naomi stood up. "How did you get to be so wise?"

"I get it from my mama." Nikki smiled. "I get my good looks from my daddy," she said, and Naomi threw a potholder at her.

As she layered sausage, ham, bacon, and spinach into the baking dish, Naomi thought about Pete's influence on her children, especially Nikki, over the years. She was so angry after Eddie's murder, so she was glad for the help and support she got from Pete and Caroline. Naomi covered the meats with shredded cheese, thinking about how Nikki and J.R. might have turned out without their intervention. She laughed to herself.

They would have turned out to be spoiled, entitled brats, she thought as she put the pan in the oven to bake for twenty-five minutes.

"Maybe he was waiting for me to have the maturity to handle it," Nikki said.

"I was just thinking the same thing. If he had let you carry that kind of power before you were ready . . ." Naomi shook her head. "It would have been bad for everyone involved. Especially you."

"I thought about that, too." Nikki laughed. "J.R. still ain't ready, to be honest with you."

"Your brother is young, so you need to keep a tight rein on that stallion."

"I'm doing my best. But it's hard to rein him in some-times."

"You can handle your brother. You always have."

"You know, before he handed me power, I was thinking about opening some legit businesses."

"What were you thinking about?"

"You know, the usual cash businesses. Laundromat, vending machine company." For reasons she couldn't understand, Nikki didn't mention opening a strip club to her mother.

Probably because she's my mother.

"But since he handed me power, I've been thinking bigger."

"Like what?"

"I was thinking about opening a restaurant. Maybe a themed restaurant like Remy runs." Nikki laughed. "That place makes so much money. It's probably why he doesn't need to skim off the top."

"There's a lot of money in food."

"How come Daddy never opened a restaurant?"

"It was something he used to talk about doing." It was her dream once. Naomi loved to cook and thought she could make it work. "But he had the Palace, and that was his pride and joy."

"I know."

"Who did you get to run the Palace?"

"Megan."

"The white girl?"

"Yes. Mommy, Megan the white girl." Nikki got up to refill her coffee. "How come you never liked Megan?"

"I don't know. Because she's white more than anything else. I don't like and have never trusted white people."

"None of them, ever?"

"Nope, never."

"I never knew."

"I really didn't see the point of imposing my racism on my children." Like she had imposed her hatred and distrust of Barlowe on Nikki. "At the very least, you deserved the right to form your own opinion about white people based on your own experiences. I didn't grow up in an area where the population is mostly white and Hispanic. I grew up in Jackson, Mississippi. It's eighty or ninety percent black." Naomi laughed. "If I didn't leave my neighborhood, I could go weeks without seeing a white person. They were our oppressors. No opportunity in that relationship for friendship."

"I see your point."

"But as far as friends are concerned, Megan has proven herself to be a real friend. I have my doubts about those other two, but Megan . . ." Naomi nodded. "She's all right."

"Sierra and Chrystal are all right, too, Mommy. You just never give them a chance."

"Where'd you put those two?"

"I got Sierra at XL, and Chrystal is running Marquee for me."

"I hope you can trust them to do what you need them to do."

Nikki laughed. "I told them 'you party girls got jobs now, so don't disappoint me.' They promised they wouldn't."

"Have you ever thought about the transport business?"

"No."

"I was reading that it is a cash-dominated business. People in urban centers use inter-city transport. These routes tend to be busy."

"Tell me about it. I used to hate to ride the bus and the train."

"But you couldn't keep your fast ass off it."

Nikki laughed. "And we'd hop the train in a heartbeat."

"You four were always going somewhere. I never knew you were hopping the train."

"What can I say? You and Uncle Pete refused to buy me a car. I had to get around somehow, and we were like, why pay when we could hop?"

"Anyway, it said that people prefer to pay these small amounts in cash in order to avoid hidden fees or hassles with the electronic apps."

"It's worth looking into."

"But I like the restaurant idea."

"I thought you might." Nikki thought it could be something they could do together. "What are you doing today?"

"I have no plans. Why?"

"I was thinking we could do some shopping and maybe look at a couple of restaurant locations while we're at it."

"Sounds good."

After breakfast, Niki and Naomi went shopping. They had a late lunch, and then they set out in search of restaurant space.

They looked at a 1,045 square-foot space. The asking price was two hundred thousand dollars. Then, it was off to a space that, due to the downtown location, was a bit more pricey at two point seven million for 2,900 square feet of space.

On the way back to Naomi's house, mother and daughter stopped for New Fu Run in Great Neck. After leaving the restaurant, Nikki got a call from Megan.

Chapter Fourteen

"Soundcheck. Team one," she said into her earpiece. It was another great addition to their program.

"Check."

"Check."

"Team two."

"Check."

Team three."

"Check."

"Check."

"Okay. Everybody knows what their job is. Let's get to it and get paid."

With that, the six left the cargo van and approached the Palace. While teams two and three went inside, the two members of team one stayed outside. Once they were in position inside the club, they checked in and prepared to make their move.

"Team two in position and standing by," one said. He and his partner had taken up a position near the edge of the dance floor.

"Team three in position and standing by." His team was in a position outside the gambling room.

"We're a go."

At that point, all three teams donned masks and made their move. The two members of team two pulled automatic weapons from under their coats and fired at the ceiling. At the same time, the members of team three rushed into the gambling room as team one hit the front door.

The customers ducked for cover, as did the unarmed security officers, who were hired to look good and keep the aisles clear. "Leave that gangster shit to them gangster niggas."

While team one took the money at the front door, team three hit the count room. Team two moved to the middle of the dance floor.

"Nobody moves, nobody gets shot!" a team member shouted, scanning the crowd with his weapon. "I need your wallets, purses, cell phone, watches, and jewelry. When my friend comes around, all you gotta do is drop them in the bag, and you get to go home alive!"

The second member of team two took out a bag and began to make her way around the crowd. When team one finished taking the front door, one member exited the Palace to prepare for their escape, while the other went inside the club, got a bag, and joined in the collection of items from the customers.

Meanwhile, in the gambling room, the bandits had taken the cash from the count room and moved on to phase two.

"Where's the manager?"

"I'm the manager," a very scared Megan said with her hands in the air.

He rushed to her and put a gun to her head. "Office! Move!" he said and shoved her toward the office. Once he got to the office with Megan, the gunman pushed her toward the safe. She stumbled to the floor in front of it.

"Open it." He tossed a bag to her. "Fill up that bag and make it quick," he said and returned the gun to the back of her head.

Megan's hand shook, and tears streamed down her cheeks as she tapped in the combination to open the safe. The gunman smiled when he saw how much cash was in there. As quickly as she could, with her hands shaking,

Megan put the money from the safe in the bag. Once the safe was empty, she handed him the bag and put her hands up.

"Don't move!" he said as he rushed out of the office.

When team three came out of the gambling room, team two was still gathering money and jewelry from the customers.

"Let's make it!" one shouted on his way to the exit. "We're coming out." The other team members stopped what they were doing and followed him out of the Palace.

Megan got to her feet and went to her desk. She picked up the phone and dialed Nikki's number.

"Hey, Megan. What's up?"

"We just got robbed."

"I'm on my way up there." Nikki ended the call and looked at Naomi. "I gotta go, Ma."

"What's wrong?"

"Somebody robbed the Palace," she said and started for the door.

"Nikki!"

"Yes, Ma."

"Be careful."

"Yes, Ma. I will," Nikki promised her mother and left the house.

The five members of the robbing crew stepped outside at the same time that Cairo and Butch arrived at the Palace. They saw the masked bandits, pulled out their guns, and began shooting. The cargo van pulled up in front of the club, and the driver jumped out of his seat to open the side panel.

"Get in!" he shouted.

The bandits ran toward the van, firing shots at Cairo and Butch. Four of them made it to the van; however, one of Cairo's shots hit the last bandit in the leg.

"We gotta go!" one shouted and closed the door. The driver drove off.

Cairo and Butch ran up to the fallen bandit and stood over him with their guns pointed. Cairo pulled off the mask.

"A woman."

"You're gonna die slow, honey," Butch said and pulled her up. "But not before you experience a lot of pain. Get up and let's go."

Chapter Fifteen

When Eddie Marx built the Palace, he included what he called the Cold Room. It was a six-by-six concrete room with no windows. The purpose of the room was torture and murder.

"Take her to the Cold Room," Butch said to Megan's men when they came out of the Palace.

It was half an hour later when Nikki arrived at the Palace and was informed that they had taken the bandit to the Cold Room.

"Where's Megan?"

"In her office."

Instead of going straight to the Cold Room, Nikki went to the office to check on her friend. Megan was seated behind her desk. She was leaning back, and her eyes were closed. Megan heard the door open, but she didn't open her eyes.

"Megan," Nikki said softly as she approached the desk.

"Yes," she said without opening her eyes.

"Are you all right?"

Megan finally opened her eyes and looked at Nikki. They were red and puffy from crying, and black mascara stained her cheeks.

"No, Nikki. I am not all right. I have never been so scared in my life."

"I know, and I'm sorry. Sorry that I put you in this position." Nikki sat down in front of Megan's desk. "I never want anything to happen to you."

"I know you don't, Nikki. I know this is the kind of thing that happens. And I knew when you put me in this position that this kind of thing could happen. At least I should have known."

"You gonna be okay?"

"Yeah. I'll be all right." Megan wiped away the tears.

"So, what happened?"

Megan shook her head. "One minute, everything is fine, and the next, two of them are in the gambling room, taking the count." She paused. "One thing."

"What's that?"

"This wasn't their first time being here. I mean, they went straight for the count room."

"I see."

"And they were on me so quick. I barely had time to think." Megan took a mirror from her desk drawer. "All I could think about was, *please don't kill me.*" She looked at herself in the mirror. "I look terrible," she said and began to redo her makeup.

"What I'm wondering is how they got the guns past the magnetometers," Nikki questioned.

"I had some thoughts about that."

"And?"

"I remember reading somewhere about something called a Faraday cage."

"A Faraday cage?"

"It's a container made of conducting material that shields what it encloses from external electric fields."

"And you think that's how they beat the magnetometers?"

"It's a possibility. That's all I'm saying, but honestly, I have no idea," Megan said as she put the finishing touches on her makeup.

Nikki stood up. "Come on. We got business to take care of."

They had installed a state-of-the-art security system, and she would be able to watch how it all went down. More importantly, it would show them how they get weapons past her state-of-the-art security system magnetometers.

"Right," Megan said, and once she put away her makeup, she followed Nikki out of the office.

They passed through the club on the way to the Cold Room. When they entered, Cairo and Butch were standing over their fallen captive. Her leg was still bleeding from the gunshot wound; therefore, she was weak from the loss of blood.

Nikki walked up to the woman and slapped her in the face. "Hey!"

The woman opened her eyes and glanced up at Nikki.

"You're gonna die tonight," Nikki began.

"I told her that," Butch said.

"But the question is how long you're gonna live before I kill you and how much pain you're willing to endure."

When she closed her eyes and turned away, Cairo punched her in the face. "Pay attention."

"Or."

Cairo punched her in the face again.

"Or you can tell me who was with you and where I find them, and I kill you quickly."

Cairo punched her in the face again.

"Your choice."

She spit blood at Nikki. "Fuck you. I ain't telling you shit," she said, and Cairo punched her in the face.

"Your choice." Nikki took out her gun and shot the woman in the other leg. She screamed in pain.

"Fuck you," she said through gritted teeth.

Nikki laughed. "No, honey, fuck you."

Nikki shot her in the stomach, and once again, the woman screamed in pain.

It was then that J.R. came into the Cold Room.

"What's going on?"

"What's up, baby brother." Nikki pointed. "Missy here and five of her best friends robbed us tonight."

"How much did they get?"

"Everything." Nikki put her foot on the gunshot wound in the woman's stomach. When she put her weight on it, the woman screamed. "They hit the front door, robbed the customers, hit the count room, and they took the safe."

J.R. glanced at Megan. "You all right?"

"Yeah, J.R., I'm fine," Megan said, and J.R. kicked the woman in the face. Then he knelt next to her.

"You need to tell her what she wants to know."

Butch laughed. "She ain't gonna talk. You might as well just kill her now," he said and put his gun to her temple.

"Who was with you, and where are they?" Nikki shouted, and she said nothing. "Where are they?" Nikki shouted again, only this time she pointed her gun at the woman's kneecap and pulled the trigger.

"Ahh, shit!" she screamed.

"Tell me where they are!" Nikki screamed and shot her in the other kneecap.

"Okay, okay! I'll tell you!"

Cliff Roffe looked out the window of the house and made note of the fact that the streetlight directly in front of the house was flickering. It was his robbing crew, so he felt responsible for Audrey Skinner getting shot and them not waiting for her. He glanced at Troy Freeman. Although he knew he was right, that they had to go, it wasn't his call to make.

He walked away from the window and approached the table where Emerson Robinson, Gregory Powers, and

Warren Cummings sat around the table, watching and waiting patiently as Freeman counted the money.

Roffe sat at the table, and Powers patted him on the back. "It couldn't be helped. We had to go."

"Easy for you to say!" Cummings shouted. He and Skinner were involved, so it was obvious that he was taking it badly. "We didn't have to leave her."

"Fuck that," Freeman said as he counted. "If we had stayed, we all could have gotten caught, or worse."

"You don't know that!" Cummings shouted.

"Kill all that noise," Roffe said. "What's done is done. Audrey knew the risk."

"Fuck you, Roffe. She wasn't your woman."

There was silence in the room as they allowed that to sink in. Roffe got up and went to sit next to Cummings. "I can't even imagine what you must be feeling now."

"No. You can't possibly know how I'm feeling."

"I'm sorry," Roffe said.

"Sorry for your loss," Powers said sympathetically. "Audrey was a good girl."

"Thanks," Cummings said.

Robinson thought he heard something. He stood up and went to the window.

"What?" Roffe asked.

"Nothing. I thought I heard something," Cummings said just as the front door burst open, and in rushed Nikki, J.R., Cairo, and Butch. They began firing at the robbers. Their first shots took out Robinson and Powers before they could reach for their guns.

Roffe quickly reached for his gun and fired at J.R., who returned his fire. The shot grazed Roffe's shoulder and hit the wall behind him. He turned and shot back at J.R., who took cover before firing back.

When the shooting started, Cummings had grabbed his gun, and he opened fire as he made a move to cover.

Nikki pulled her guns and dove for the floor, while Butch fired and hit Cummings with two to the head.

Freeman turned over the table and kept firing at Cairo. He raised his weapon and shot back, but he missed. Butch stayed low and moved to get a better angle on the shooter. When he was in position, he fired and took Freeman out. When Freeman went down, that gave Nikki her chance, and she came up and blasted at Roffe. He fired at her, and she was forced to take cover. Then she stood up and hit Roffe with two shots to the chest.

Now that the shooting had ended, Cairo and Butch gathered up all the money on the table, and the four left the house.

Chapter Sixteen

The Complex was a massive outdoor venue featuring a sunken dance floor, with live shows and a DJ that spun the hits until the sun came up the following day. The spot featured a sensory-overloading laser and LED light show. On any given night, you might see some of the biggest artists on the music and entertainment scene. The three-level location housed a restaurant and a nightclub. The restaurant was on the ground floor, with the nightclub on the upper floor. In the basement, which was a network of brick tunnels, there were a couple of bars and lounge areas. That night, the hotspot was where Shekita and Rah-Rah were hanging out at happy hour with Shekira's girlfriend, Omeika.

"This place is nice," Omeika said.

"Is this your first time coming here?" Rah-Rah asked.

"It is," Omeika said, dancing in her chair to the beat. "But it won't be my last time. I promise you that."

"I'm glad you came," Shekira said. "It's been so long since we hung out."

"The job. You know how it is."

"What do you do, Omeika?" Rah-Rah asked. Omeika was Shekira's friend, so she felt left out of their side conversations. She was thinking about making up some excuse and calling Cairo.

"I'm a software engineer for MTS. I do hands-on coding and unit-testing projects for the engineering team." She sipped her drink. "What about you, Rah-Rah?"

"I'm a dancer in music videos," she replied, even though she had only done one video, and she hadn't heard from Thatcher since then. She had gotten an agent, so she hoped to get more work.

"Oh," Omeika said excitedly. "That must be very exciting. I mean, the people I'm sure you've met."

"Yeah, I meet famous people all the time," Rah-Rah claimed, even though the shoot she was in was just dancers, and she didn't meet anybody famous. The truth was that it was one day's work. She didn't make that much money, and what she did make was going fast.

"When was the last time we hung out?" Shekira asked.

"Oh, it's been at least a year, more than that now that I'm thinking about it." She paused to think. "It was that afterparty for Salomé Warner's at Boom on East Forty-eighth."

"Sure was. Damn, girl, it has been a while."

"Like I said, work, work, work. Them paying me makes them think they own my mind, body, and my time."

"Seems like they do," Shekira quipped.

"I think you're right." Omeika laughed. "So tonight, I'm gonna have some fun."

"That's right," Shekira encouraged.

"Let yourself go tonight. Do something you normally wouldn't," Rah-Rah suggested.

"That right, because tomorrow morning, you'll be right there coding."

"I sure will." Omeika nodded. "I'm gonna have some fun tonight," she said, and for the next hour, the three drank and danced and had a good time.

When they got back to their table from the dance floor, Shekira noticed that she had a missed call. She called him back right away.

"What's up, J.R.?"

"How you doing, Shekira?"

"Sorry I missed your call. Me, Rah-Rah, and a girlfriend who I haven't seen in ages." Shekira and Omeika high-fived, and Rah-Rah rolled her eyes. "We're hanging out at the Complex. You should come hang out with us."

"Text me the address, and I'll meet you there."

"I'm sending the address now," Shekira said, sending her location. "See you when you get here."

"Who was that?" Rah-Rah asked.

"J.R. He's gonna meet us here," Shekira said, and Rah-Rah wondered if Cairo would be with him.

"Who's J.R.?" Omeika asked.

"He's just a guy I know," Shekira said, minimizing the extent of her relationship with J.R.

Knowing how into J.R. Shekira actually was, Rah-Rah rolled her eyes and looked away. "You'll like J.R. He's nice," she said.

"So," Omeika said. "You ladies ready for another round?"

"I am," Shekira said and signaled for a server. When one arrived, he took their orders and disappeared. J.R., Cairo, and Butch arrived at the table shortly after that.

"What's up, ladies?" J.R. asked as he slid into the booth next to Shekira.

"Hey," Shekira all but giggled.

"What up, Rah-Rah?"

"You know me. Doing what I do," Rah-Rah replied, but she was looking at Cairo. He winked at her.

"J.R., this is my friend, Omeika."

"J.R. Marx."

"Nice to meet you."

Cairo leaned close to J.R. "We gonna go do that thing," he said.

"You want us to come back for you?" Butch asked.

He glanced at Shekira. She puckered her pouty lips. "I'm good."

"We'll get with you," Cairo said, and he and Butch turned to leave.

"Let me holla at you before you go, Cairo," Rah-Rah said and stood up.

"Come on then. We gotta go," Cairo said and kept walking. He knew what Rah-Rah wanted. She was getting to be a steady customer.

Cairo stopped when he got outside. "What you need?"

She leaned close to him. "You got an eightball?" she asked softly, looking around.

"Powder or rock?"

"Rock. I can't cook."

Cairo laughed and started for the car. "You need to learn how to cook."

"Maybe you should teach me."

"All you gotta do is come around," Cairo said as he got to his car. He opened the door and sat in the passenger seat while he went into the glove compartment.

"Come on, man! We gotta go!" Butch shouted from his car.

"Here you go," Cairo said and got out. "I'll get with you later," he said and rushed to get in the car with Butch.

Rah-Rah stood there and watched them drive off, thinking about walking straight to her car and going home to smoke, but she knew she needed to go back inside and say something to Shekira. She went back inside, knowing that she couldn't just go in there, make up some excuse, and leave. It would look funny if she did that, so Rah-Rah sat there for the next half hour, and then she said, "I got an audition in the morning, so I'm gonna get outta here."

"You gotta go?" Shekira asked. She thought it was strange that Rah-Rah hadn't said anything about an audition. But Rah-Rah had been acting secretive lately. Shekira planned to ask her about it the next time she saw Rah-Rah.

Rah-Rah stood up. "Yeah, I gotta go. I wanna get some sleep."

"Okay." Shekira got up and hugged her. "I was thinking about getting outta here soon, too."

"You all right?"

"Yeah, I'm all right," Shekira said, but she felt like she had a migraine coming on.

"I'll call you tomorrow," Rah-Rah said and broke their embrace.

"Let me know how it went."

"It was nice to meet you, Omeika."

"Same here," Omeika said, and Rah-Rah left the Complex.

Shekira sat down. "Honestly, Omeika, I was thinking about calling it a night, too. I feel a migraine coming on."

"I'm sorry," Omeika said and finished her drink.

"You leaving already?" J.R. asked. "I just got here."

"I know. And I'm sorry, but I feel a migraine coming on. You understand, don't you?"

"Yeah, I understand," J.R. said, but he was disappointed. The only reason he was there was that Shekira was extraordinary in bed.

I could have gone with Cairo and Butch.

"Thank you for understanding, J.R. I promise to make it up to you." Shekira looked at Omeika. "That doesn't mean you have to go. You haven't been out, and God only knows when you'll get out again."

"You sure?"

"Yes, I'm sure. Have a good time and enjoy yourself." She laughed. "What did Rah-Rah say? Let yourself go tonight. Do something you usually wouldn't do." Shekira turned to J.R., "Make sure my friend has a good time and enjoys herself."

"Okay," J.R. said and looked at Omeika. "It will be my pleasure."

"Don't let it be a year before I hear from you again," Shekira said.

"I promise. It won't," Omeika said, and Shekira left J.R. and Omeika alone at the Complex.

"Come dance with me," Omeika said when a new song began.

"Let's go," J.R. said and followed Omeika out on the floor. They danced with their drinks in hands. When they finished their drinks, J.R. discarded the empty glasses on the nearest table and went back to dancing with Omeika. They stayed out there for a long time, smiling, laughing, and having a good time. By the time they left the floor, they were both drenched.

They went back to the bar, and J.R. ordered another round of drinks. While they drank, they talked about the time they'd just spent on the dance floor and what a good time they were having together.

"You're quite the dancer," Omeika flirted.

"So are you."

"I feel very comfortable dancing with you." She moved a little closer to J.R. "Like we've known each other and have been dancing for years."

"Yeah, I felt that too," J.R. said, and they stared into each other's eyes.

"Come on. Let's dance," Omeika said quickly and grabbed J.R.'s hand. She led him back onto the dance floor.

J.R. and Omeika spent the rest of the night dancing, drinking, and talking about any and everything. When the Complex closed in the morning, they drifted out with the crowd.

"Did you enjoy yourself?" J.R. asked.

"I did. I had a good time with you."

"Do you have a ride home?"

"I was going to call an Uber."

"So was I. You wanna share?"

"Sure," Omeika said, taking out her phone to access the app. When the Uber arrived, they rode to Omeika's apartment. "You wanna come up?"

"I really do," J.R. said quickly, getting out of the Uber with Omeika.

Omeika quickly stepped out of her pumps, and as soon as they were in her apartment, she stepped to his chest and put her arms around him. J.R. kissed her. His mouth on hers was absolutely fantastic. She was wet and eager to have him inside of her. His tongue action, the way their lips caressed each other's. The way his hands moved across her pebbled skin made her feel alive and wanting as their lips parted.

Omeika put her arms around him, and they kissed again. His kisses were hot, demanding, and intense. They were everything she'd fantasized about for years. Omeika could feel his strong hands at her back, easing down her zipper, sliding her dress off her shoulders, and allowing it to drop to the floor. Omeika felt his hands all over her body, and then J.R. spread her legs a little bit and began gliding his hand tenderly into her drenched mound. She gasped when J.R. slid her thong to one side and massaged her clit. Omeika felt as if she would come apart right then.

J.R. took one of her nipples in his mouth as he continued to finger her clit. It sent waves of pleasure through her body. He kissed his way down her stomach, and then he got on his knees, spread her lips, and tasted her. Omeika was in ecstasy as J.R. worked his magic tongue. Omeika held on to his head and prayed that he wouldn't stop.

J.R. kissed his way back up her trembling body and laid her across the bed. It took a while to adjust to his size. His thrusts were hard, but he was hitting her spots like he knew where each place was. His strokes were deep, so deep that Omeika could feel him all up in her stomach.

Chapter Seventeen

Hey, Shekira, it's Omeika. I just wanted to say how good it was to see you. And I promise, it definitely won't be a year before we do it again. Thank you for insisting that I stay, and thank you so much for insisting that J.R. take care of me. My body feels fantastic. Talk soon.

It was turning out to be a good day for J.R. He got home after six in the morning, woke up in the afternoon, and spent the next couple of hours watching reruns of Perry Mason before he got out of bed and hit the shower.

When he left the apartment, J.R. went to Clay's garage to shoot craps with a couple of old friends from high school. While he was there, the houseman, Mitchell, got into it with a man who claimed they were playing with loaded dice. When the man pulled a gun on Mitchell, J.R. grabbed the gun and threw the man out the front door.

When he left the crap with a pocket full of money, he was riding by Marquee and was surprised to see his mother's car parked down the street from the hotel. More curious about what she was doing there in the middle of the day than anything else, J.R. parked the car and went inside. Happy Hour was winding down, and the cook had just restocked the buffet with mini pizzas, crab cakes, egg rolls, buffalo wings, and mac and cheese bites with bacon bits.

Since he hadn't eaten all day, J.R. got a plate and helped himself before going to the office to look for his mother. When he got to the office, he found his mother was in there with Nikki and Chrystal.

"Hey, Ma," J.R. said and sat down to eat. "What are you doing here?" he asked with his mouth full.

"Your sister's been thinking about opening a restaurant, and we've been out looking at some places," Naomi said.

"Why didn't you call me?"

"For what?" Nikki asked.

"To see if I wanted to go with y'all."

"Why? You never have wanted to do stuff like that with me and Mommy before."

"Maybe that's true. But it still would have been nice to be asked."

"Whatever, J.R.," Nikki said with a dismissive wave of her hand.

"Now, now, Nikki. Your brother is right. When you and I do things as a family, we should, at the very least, give him an opportunity."

"Opportunity for what, Mommy? To say he's too busy between some woman's thighs to be bothered with us?"

"Unfair. True, but unfair," J.R. said, and Chrystal laughed.

"See." Nikki pointed at her brother.

"If your sister is right, you should do something about it."

"Okay. Next time y'all go looking for a place, call me, and I will make time to meet y'all there."

"No need," Nikki said, smiling.

"Why is that?"

"Because," Nikki began, "baby brother, we found a spot we like, and we're going to make an offer on it."

"That's great."

"It's a newly renovated retail building with more than thirty-eight hundred square feet of space. The building spans two floors and has a fully built roof deck area."

"Location?" J.R. questioned.

"It's in a busy business corridor, with a lot of foot traffic," Naomi informed, "And it's close to major subway lines."

Nikki looked at her watch. "It's not far from here if you wanna see it."

"Sure. Let's go." He stood up. "Wait."

"What?" Naomi asked.

"Ain't it too late to look at the space?"

"No. Your sister has the code to get in," Naomi said, following Nikki to the door. "You coming or not?"

"Coming."

The three went to the potential restaurant, and Naomi showed J.R. around while Nikki shared her vision for the place.

"What type of food are you thinking about serving?" J.R. asked.

"American food," Nikki said. "Burgers, fries, pizza, hot dogs, fried chicken, shrimp, mac and cheese, and BBQ ribs."

"That should do good in this spot." J.R. and Naomi went and sat down at the table with Nikki. "Now, this is just me playing devil's advocate, but what do either of you know about running a restaurant?"

Nikki and Naomi glanced at one another. "Nothing. But Chrystal used to manage an Arby's."

"Before she got fired," J.R. reminded them.

"Why did she get fired?" Naomi wanted to know.

"She was the scapegoat for a bad inspection. Somebody had to go, and she was the newest manager on duty."

"I know how that goes. But you got her running Marquee. She gonna do both?"

"No. But when the time comes, she'll make the move, and we'll hire somebody else to manage Marquee," Nikki said.

"By the time we're ready to open this place for business, Chrystal should have trained an assistant to take over for her," Naomi said.

"Sounds like you plan on being hands-on in this venue, Ma."

"No more than I am in any of your other businesses," Naomi said, and Nikki reacted immediately.

"That is not what we talked about, Mommy."

"What did y'all talk about?" J.R. asked, feeling somewhat left out.

"Now that the two of you are taking a more active role in controlling the businesses, your sister thought that it would be a good idea for me to, you know, keep an eye on the money."

J.R. chuckled. "You don't trust Uncle Pete and Arya."

"Never have, never will," Naomi said.

Nikki stood up, smiling. "Makes her perfect for the job, don't it?"

"It does," J.R. agreed. He never did understand his mother's distrust and flat-out hatred of Uncle Pete after all he'd done for them.

"Now, I know you stuffed yourself on the buffet at the club, but I'm hungry," Nikki said.

"I could eat again."

"You should have known that, Nikki. The boy has two stomachs." Naomi laughed as she followed her children out of the restaurant space.

"What do you have a taste for?" J.R. asked on the way to the car.

"I've been craving some Thai food lately," Nikki said.

"There's a Thai joint just opened up not far from here," Naomi informed them.

"What's it called?"

"Thai LumLum."

At Thai LumLum, Nikki had tempura-battered jumbo shrimp on a bed of broccoli covered with chili sauce. It was pork garlic and pepper stir-fry for Naomi, and J.R. had the Thai bell pepper steak. After they ate, Naomi drove her children back to Marquee before heading home for the evening.

Nikki and J.R. were sitting in a booth at Marquee with Chrystal, Cairo, and Butch. They were enjoying the music of the band Future Shock. They were on stage doing a medley of old Impressions and Curtis Mayfield songs. It was right about that time when J.R. saw Shekira and Rah-Rah come into Marquee. He watched her as she looked around the club, and once they made eye contact, Shekira's eyes narrowed, and she headed straight for the table.

"What's up, Shekira?" J.R. asked.

"Can I talk to you for a minute?"

J.R. stood up as Shekira turned away from the table. "Be right back."

Once she was away from the table, Shekira turned to face J.R.

"Why did you fuck my girlfriend?" Shekira shouted over the music, and it got everyone's attention.

Shekira had been asleep when Omeika left that message. When she woke up, she didn't check her messages until late that afternoon. Then, she read the message twice to be sure of what it said. Then she called Omeika.

"Hey, girl."

"You fucked J.R.?"

"I did, and it was so good," Omeika swooned.

"Why would you do that?"

"Did I do something wrong?"

"You fucked my man. That's what you did wrong."

"Your man? I didn't know. The way you made it seem was as if he was just some guy you knew, and you were hooking me up."

"No, Omeika. Whatever gave you that idea?"

"You said, 'He's nice. You'll like him.' Then, when he got there, you and Rah-Rah left. Then you encouraged me to stay, and you insisted that he show me a good time. And then you left me alone with him."

"That was not what I wanted," Shekira said angrily, ending the call. Since this was a conversation she wanted to have in person, Shekira had been hunting J.R. ever since. She'd been riding with Rah-Rah, going from spot to spot until she found him at Marquee.

J.R. took a step back. "What?" he asked, but he had heard what she said.

"Why did you fuck my girlfriend?" Shekira screamed.

"She told you? I can't believe she told you that shit."

"Yes, she told me!" Shekira swung at him.

Cairo and Butch stood up.

"Why did you fuck my girlfriend?"

"It just kinda happened," J.R. said, taking another step backward.

Shekira's eyes narrowed, and she nodded her head. "Just kinda happened, my ass, muthafucka!"

She dug in her purse. When she pulled out a knife and swung it at him, Nikki bounced up.

"Muthafucka, I'll kill you!" Shekira shouted and swung the knife at him again.

Nikki stepped to her quickly and put the barrel of her gun to Shekira's head. "Drop the knife, or I will blow your fuckin' head off."

Shekira froze, and then she dropped the knife. Nikki moved the gun away. When she did, Shekira rushed at J.R., and Butch grabbed her.

"Get her outta here," Nikki said, and Butch carried Shekira, kicking and screaming, to the exit.

"You all right?" Nikki asked J.R.

He sat down at the table. "Yeah, I'm all right."

Nikki sat down next to him. "You fucked her friend?"

J.R. nodded.

She shook her head. "I keep telling you that dick gonna be the death of you."

"Yeah, maybe. But not today," J.R. said as Rah-Rah approached Cairo.

"Let me holla at you, Cairo," Rah-Rah said.

"What you need?"

She leaned close to him. "I want an eightball, but I'm a little short," she whispered.

Cairo looked at Rah-Rah and thought about how badly he wanted to fuck her. "No worries, sexy. I got you. Come on," Cairo said, and Rah-Rah followed him out to his car.

Chapter Eighteen

Naomi came down the stairs, but instead of entering the kitchen, she went into the living room and looked out the window. As it had been for the last few weeks, Nikki's car was parked in the driveway. Naomi went to the kitchen to start breakfast and make coffee, wondering what was going on with her daughter.

"You know, the one who couldn't wait to move out of the house," she said aloud.

She knew it had to be something, but she didn't want to pry into Nikki's personal life. All she could do was hope it wasn't serious and Nikki would tell her about it when she was ready.

As it had the past few mornings, the smell of bacon cooking awakened Nikki. She got out of bed and dragged herself into the kitchen.

"Good morning, Mommy," Nikki said, getting a coffee cup from the cabinet.

"Morning, Nikki. How are you this morning?"

"I'm fine. How are you?" Nikki asked, sitting down at the table.

"I can't complain. Wouldn't do any good if I did."

"What could you possibly have to complain about, Mommy? You truly are the woman who has everything."

"Material things. I got plenty of that. But having money doesn't mean you're happy."

"Are you happy?"

"Like I said, I have nothing to complain about. I live a good life. I have children who not only love me but still wanna be bothered with me. And believe me, all parents can't say that."

"Of course we love you, Mommy."

"And you want me to be a part of your world. That means a lot to me," Naomi said as Nikki's cell phone began to ring. She glanced at the display and saw that it was Barlowe calling.

"Hello."

"Morning, Nikki. Sorry to be calling so early, but I need to see you and J.R. this morning."

"I'm at my mom's house having breakfast, but as soon as I'm done, I'll round up J.R., and we'll be out there."

"See you when you get here. And say hello to your mom for me."

"Will do," Nikki said, ending the call. "Barlowe said to tell you hello."

Naomi rolled her eyes and put a plate in front of Nikki. "What does he want?"

"He wants to see me and J.R. at the house."

After finishing breakfast with her mother, Nikki called J.R. and told him to meet her at Barlowe's house. Then she headed for the shower.

Later that morning, when J.R. arrived at Barlowe's house, Reggie escorted him to the library where Arya was waiting. When Reggie closed the door, Arya allowed the Josie Natori lucky dragon silk long robe she was wearing to drop to the floor. She stood naked before him.

"Come on. We don't have a lot of time."

J.R. thought about what had happened the night before with Shekira and what Nikki had been saying about his dick getting him killed. J.R. shook his head. "We can't do this, Arya. Not anymore."

"Can't? Why can't we?"

Arya moved closer and rested her tits on him. She looked up into his eyes, and he pushed her away. "Because I'm not a scared little boy anymore. I'm not scared that if I don't do everything you say, you'll tell Uncle Pete." He took another step backward. "Well, go ahead and tell him. Tell him how you sucked my dick in the pool house. And how many times you fucked me in his bed. And about how you fucked me on the table where he eats his food. Then you can tell him about how much you loved to fuck me while I sat in the chair where he likes to do his drinking. Tell him. I think it will go a whole lot worse for you than it does for me. I gotta go. Nikki will be here soon."

Arya picked up her robe and put it back on just as Barlowe and Nikki were coming into the library.

"Morning, J.R.," Barlowe said when he came in.

"What's up, Uncle Pete?"

"What did you want to see us about?" Nikki asked as an angry Arya stormed out of the room, slamming the door behind her.

"What did you say to her?" Barlowe asked J.R.

"I told her no."

Barlowe laughed. "She doesn't like to be told no."

"What did you want to see us about?" Nikki asked again to get the men back on task.

"I need the two of you to collect from Huxley."

When Nikki and J.R. arrived at Huxley's apartment, they knocked on the door, and to their surprise, Huxley opened the door.

"Surprised to see us?" J.R. said, pushing him inside. "Barlowe sent us for his money."

"I don't have it," Huxley said as he regained his footing.

"What you mean, you ain't got it?" Nikki asked, and J.R. punched him in the chest. Huxley stumbled backward.

"I mean I don't have it here." Huxley coughed and backed up.

"I'm getting tired of this shit, Huxley." Nikki patted his cheek. J.R. punched Huxley in the stomach, and the blow doubled him over.

"Look at me when I'm talking to you," Nikki said.

J.R. punched Huxley in the stomach again, and once again, the blow doubled him over.

"I'm gonna ask you one more time, and if you don't tell me what I wanna hear,"—Nikki got in his face—"I'm just gonna let J.R. beat the fuck outta you."

J.R. got in his face to say, "And I wanna beat the shit outta you."

"Where is the money?"

"In my pocket," Huxley said. He held up one hand and slowly reached into his pocket, pulled out the money, and handed it to Nikki.

"Thank you." Nikki patted Huxley on the cheek and walked away.

J.R. punched him in the stomach. "Should have done that when she asked you the first time," J.R. said and punched him in the stomach again.

When J.R. and Nikki left the apartment and closed the door, men got off the elevator and started toward them.

"Oh, shit," Nikki said quietly.

"What?" J.R. asked.

"That's Huxley's crew," Nikki said as they passed.

Once the men reached Huxley's apartment, they went inside.

J.R. pushed the button for the elevator, but that was when Huxley's apartment door opened, and armed men came pouring out.

"Oh, shit!" Nikki said, and then she and J.R. took off running for the stairwell.

As they ran down the stairs, two men entered the stairwell and began firing. Nikki and J.R. were able to make it out of the building, across the street, and behind a car. Nikki raised up and tried to get a shot off, but she realized she was seriously outgunned and quickly dropped back behind the car to avoid being hit by the barrage of flying bullets. J.R. opened fire and promptly dropped back behind the vehicle.

But then, the shooting stopped. J.R. peeked around the car and saw two men circling around. He nodded at Nikki, and they prepared to engage their attackers head-on. J.R. stood up and fired on his man until his gun was empty, and he went down. When he did, Nikki stood up quickly and killed the other man as he advanced.

Chapter Nineteen

In three very different parts of the city, three very different women were getting ready to go see a man. One, because she was in love. The second was going out of desperation, and the other was going to get revenge.

Francine stood in front of her closet, trying to decide what to wear. At first, she thought about wearing the red and white Milly Liv Grand Foliage rib-knit dress and a cute pair of white Bottega Veneta mules. However, once she thought about it, she decided the outfit was too much for where she planned to say she was going. Therefore, instead of the dress, Francine chose a pair of Area crystal-embellished straight-leg jeans and the jacket that she wore with her favorite Christian Louboutin pumps. Now that she had selected her outfit, Francine got in the shower.

Meanwhile, in the living room, Remy and two of his men, Hakeem and Jace, were talking about their positions and the future. Both were affected by Nikki's sudden rise to power.

"Something on your mind?" Hakeem asked.

"Why you ask?" Remy asked.

"That I-got-shit-on-my-mind look on your face."

"Is it that obvious?"

"Yeah," Jace said. "You look like some major shit about to happen."

"I was thinking about Nikki."

"What about her?" Hakeem asked.

"I wasn't expecting Barlowe to hand her power like that."

"I'm surprised too," Jace cosigned. "I thought Barlowe was the kind of muthafucka that would wanna hold on to his power until he dies."

"I did, too, because that's the kind of muthafucka he is. He must have had a good reason to just give it up like that."

"Maybe he's dying."

"Maybe. But either way, live or dying, Nikki and what she's gonna do is the problem."

"Why do you say that?" Jace asked.

"You remember that night Nikki and J.R. came around talking about how Barlowe wanted us to tighten up on the money?"

"Yeah, what about it?" Hakeem asked.

"I talked to Nikki that night about what would happen if and when Barlowe retired." Remy chuckled. "Or somebody retired him. And we talked about working together. The next thing you know, Nikki's carrying all the power. She must have gone straight to him and convinced him to hand her power."

"What does that mean for you?" Jace asked.

"I don't know. I ain't seen or heard from her or J.R. since they took over."

"Worst case?"

"Worst case, they try to cut us out. In that case, I got a couple of directions to go in."

"Best case?"

"Best case scenario is the beat goes on with interruption. To me, that's the smart play. I make them niggas too much money for the shit to go any other way. But my sainted grandmother told me that it's a poor rat that only has one hole."

"No disrespect to Grandma, but what the fuck does that mean?" Hakeem asked.

"It means to always have a backup plan in case the sun don't shine your way that day."

"So, what's yours?" Jace asked.

"We work on two paths at the same time. We keep doing business as usual, but at the same time, we pursue other options."

"And if one of those options works better for us?" Hakeem asked.

"Then we make a change," Remy said as Francine came down the stairs. The men got quiet.

"You look nice. Where are you going?" Remy asked.

"To see my mother," Francine said, and she kissed Remy on the cheek.

"Tell her I said hello."

"I will." Francine moved toward the door. "You want me to bring you anything when I come back?"

"That depends."

"On?"

"What are you cooking when you get home?"

"I was thinking about picking up something. What do you have a taste for?"

"Why don't you stop and get something from that Mediterranean place?"

"You want me to get you the lamb kofta terra cotta?"

"That's what I got the last time?"

"Yes."

"Then that's what I want," Remy said.

"I'll be back in a couple of hours," Francine said, and she was out the door.

At that same time, Arya was contemplating what she should wear to accomplish her purpose. She wasn't used to being told no, but that was precisely what J.R. had told her: "No, we can't do this anymore." That was indeed the last thing that she had expected to hear from him. She thought that he enjoyed it and looked forward to their secret hook-ups as much as she did.

Being wrong—about anything—was something else she wasn't used to. And besides, she wasn't mistaken, not about this. J.R. did want her. He just needed to be reminded. Therefore, Arya selected an Oscar de la Renta floral embroidered minidress, and her pretty feet were adorned with a pair of Stuart Weitzman ankle-strap stiletto sandals and a Stuart Weitzman stellar crescent suede crossbody bag.

"You look nice," Barlowe said when he saw her in the foyer. "Where are you going?"

"Shopping," Arya said, and she kissed Barlowe on the cheek.

"You shop too much."

"You like me to look nice for you, don't you, baby?"

"I do."

"Well, this is how I do it." Arya moved toward the door. "You want me to bring anything when I come back?"

"No. But don't be too long. We have dinner reservations at the Kailash Grill House at seven."

"Don't worry. I'll be back long before that," Arya said, but if she was successful, she planned to make it last.

Arya left the house, got in her car, and drove to J.R.'s apartment.

Shekira arrived at J.R.'s apartment and parked down the street. She put her gun in her purse and put on a big hat and sunglasses. Shekira got out, and with her head down, she walked to J.R.'s apartment.

When she got to the door, J.R. had just opened the door and stepped outside. He had his gun in his hand. His sudden appearance startled her, and she froze. Shekira's plan had been to have her weapon ready when she rang the bell. When J.R. opened the door, she would shoot and kill him.

What now? she asked herself.

"What are you doing here?"

Shekira said nothing, still frozen by her fear.

"You need to get the fuck outta here." J.R. pointed the gun in her face. "Before I shoot you."

Shekira turned and began walking away quickly.

"If I ever see you again, I'll kill you!"

J.R. stood outside the apartment and watched Shekira until she was out of sight.

Francine parked the car in front of the building and got out. On her way to the apartment, she walked right past Shekira.

Arya arrived in time to see the two women pass each other. She recognized Francine right away. As Francine continued walking toward the apartment, Arya sat in her car, fuming, and then she saw the door to J.R.'s apartment open, and he came out. As Francine got closer to him, J.R. walked quickly to meet her.

"That bitch."

Arya took out her phone and began to take pictures of Francine as she rushed into J.R.'s arms, and they kissed. Arya kept clicking off photos as the two hugged and kissed, until the apartment door closed. Arya looked at the pictures she'd taken, and then she dialed a number.

"Arya, what's up with you?" Remy asked.

"Just wondering where Francine is."

"Francine? She's at her mother's house. Why?"

"I'm going to send you a text. Call me back when you get it," Arya said and ended the call.

She quickly attached the best images to the text and sent it to Remy. It took him two minutes to call back.

"That fuckin' bitch."

"I just thought you needed to know."

"Yeah, right. That's the niggas apartment. What were you doing there?"

"I was just in the area."

"Bullshit! You fuckin' that nigga too. But we'll let that pass for now."

"The question is, what are you gonna do about it?"

"Don't you worry your pretty little head about that, Arya. I got something for J.R.'s ass."

"You need to let me help you. Unless you want Nikki coming after you."

"No. I do not."

"I didn't think so."

"So, tell me, what did you have in mind?"

"A trap."

"I'm listening," Remy said, and he then listened as Arya laid out her plan for both of them to get revenge. "I can do that."

"If you can do that, you leave the rest to me," Arya said and ended the call. She put her phone back in her purse, and then, to keep up appearances, she went shopping.

Almost two hours later, Francine came out of J.R.'s apartment. He walked her to the car, and after a long and passionate kiss, she got in her car. She stopped at the Mediterranean place and picked up the lamb kofta terra cotta for Remy and an order of beef shawarma for herself, then headed home.

Since Hakeem's and Jace's cars were still parked in the driveway, Francine parked on the grass and went in the back door. As she was passing the living room to go upstairs, she overheard a conversation.

"She's gonna get Barlowe to send J.R. to collect some money from Cromwell, but it's a trap," Francine heard Remy tell Jace and Hakeem. "Cromwell died of an overdose in Milwaukee somewhere."

"What did you say?" Francine asked when she came into the living room.

Remy looked up at her. "Y'all excuse us."

"Sure," Jace said and got up. He left the room with Hakeem.

"I'll get with you tomorrow," Remy said as he walked them to the door. Once he closed the door, he turned to Francine with anger in his eyes.

"You think I'm stupid." He slapped her.

Francine grabbed her face. "What are you talking about?" Tears began to roll down her cheeks.

Remy slapped her again. "I know you're fuckin' J.R. behind my back!" he shouted.

Francine went down from the force of the blow. "What are you talking about?" she asked through her tears.

Remy pulled her up by the hair and shoved the phone in her face. "This what I'm talking about. You! Hugged up and kissing this nigga." He slapped her again.

Francine fell to the floor and crawled away. When she saw him coming, Francine struggled to get to her feet.

"I oughta kill you," he shouted.

Francine threw a lamp at Remy, and she ran out the back door.

"Come back here!" he yelled and ran behind her.

She made it to her car, unlocked the door, and started it up as Remy made it there. He began banging on the window.

"Open the fuckin' door!" Remy shouted.

Francine's hands were shaking when she put the car in reverse.

"Open the fuckin' door!" he screamed.

She backed away from the house with Remy running alongside the vehicle, banging on the window. She almost hit him when she backed into the street and then turned to drive away.

"You bring your lying, cheating ass back here, you fuckin' bitch!" Remy screamed, taking out his gun and firing off a few shots that hit nothing.

Chapter Twenty

The following day, Arya put her plan into action. She made a point of spending the day on the phone, talking to contacts and the people she generally gossiped with, so Barlowe could see her. Then she faked this call:

"What up, Cromwell?" she said and then paused as if she were listening to what he had to say. "I don't know why he's not answering his phone," she said, followed by more silence. "He'll be glad to hear that. I'll let him know. Talk to you soon."

"Who was that?"

"Cromwell."

"What he want?"

"He says he got your money and wants you to send somebody to meet him at the Red Hook Houses tonight at eight."

"About fuckin' time."

"I know. But he said he included an extra ten grand for making you wait so long for your money."

"The least he could do." Barlowe got up and went to the bar in his library. "Get J.R. on the phone and ask him to stop by. Tell him I got work for him." Barlowe laughed as he poured a drink, "The kind of work he likes."

Arya smiled at how well it was going and took out her phone. She knew that Cromwell was nowhere to be found, the perfect one to set up. Arya knew for a fact that Cromwell had left the city a month ago and was hiding out in Chicago from somebody else he owed money. She was able to verify that he was still in the wind before she made her fake call. She had no idea that Cromwell was dead.

"What you want?" J.R. asked when he answered.

"Barlowe wants to see you."

"Tell Uncle Pete I'm on my way," J.R. said quickly and hung up before Arya could say another word.

"He's on his way," Arya said with an immense feeling of satisfaction.

It was an hour later when Arya looked out the window and saw J.R.'s car pull into the driveway. She watched him get out.

Reggie let him in and escorted J.R. to the library, where Barlowe was waiting with Arya.

"What's up, Uncle Pete?"

"I'm all right. Listen, I got something important I want you to do for me."

"What's that?"

"You remember Cromwell?"

"Yeah, I remember that deadbeat. I hear he was in the wind."

"Yeah, well, he surfaced today and says he's ready to pay what he owes. Once you get money, you make sure he understands the error of his ways, and you make sure that he feels it deep in his bones. Understood?"

"Understood. You want him dead or just bleeding?"

"Bleeding badly will do."

"Where and when?"

"At the Red Hook Houses tonight at eight."

"No problem," J.R. said, and he left the house on his way to the Red Hook Houses for the trap Remy and Arya had set for him.

On his way, he took out his phone and called Cairo. "Where you at?"

"XL. What's up?"

"I'm on my way there to pick you up. We got work to put in."

"I'll be waiting," Cairo said.

When J.R. arrived at XL, he went inside, and not seeing Cairo right away, he went to the bar to get a drink.

"What's up, J.R.?" Cairo asked, walking up behind him. "You ready?"

"Yeah." J.R. shot the drink, and then he left XL with Cairo.

At 7:57 sharp, J.R. and Cairo arrived at the Red Hook Houses.

"You know which building he's in?" Cairo asked of the thirty-building complex.

"This one," J.R. said as he parked the car. "Let's go."

The second J.R. stepped out of the car, the shooting started. The first shot hit him in the head, and he fell to the ground.

"Oh, shit!" Cairo shouted, taking cover behind the car.

There were five more shots, but then it was quiet. Cairo got to his feet slowly and came around the car, carefully looking in all directions with his weapon raised. He saw J.R. lying on the ground with a pool of blood forming around his head.

"Oh, shit! Oh, shit!" He picked up his friend. Knowing that he definitely wouldn't survive waiting for an ambulance, Cairo put J.R. in the car and rushed him to the hospital. He called Nikki on the way.

"What's up, Cairo?"

"J.R.'s been shot. I'm taking him to the hospital."

However, by the time Nikki arrived, the doctors had pronounced him dead.

Chapter Twenty-one

When Nikki and Butch arrived at the hospital, they saw Cairo sitting with his head in the palms of his hands. His eyes were red and puffy when he looked up at them.

Cairo shook his head. "He didn't make it."

Nikki gasped. "What?"

"They shot him in the head, Nikki. Wasn't anything they could do."

Nikki's knees got weak, and Butch had to catch her before she fell. She began to cry. Butch led her to a seat, and Nikki sat down.

"He's dead. J.R. is dead. I can't believe it," Nikki cried, and Cairo put his arm around her to try to comfort her.

"I'm sorry. I got him here as fast as I could," Cairo said, and a tear drifted down his cheek. He and J.R. had been friends since elementary school.

"I know you did."

The three sat there in silence, with each one thinking about J.R. and what he meant to them.

"I can't sit here." Nikki bounced up and wiped away her tears. "I need to tell my mother."

"Come on," Butch said. "I'll drive you."

The silence continued in the car on the way to Naomi's house. There was no music playing, and no one said a word. Nikki sat in the back seat with tears streaming down her cheeks. She was trying to think of the right words to tell her mother that her son was dead.

It was late when they arrived at the house, so Nikki had to wake her mother up to tell her the devastating news.

"He's dead. J.R. is dead, Mommy."

"What?" Noami asked as tears formed in the corners of her eyes. "What did you say?" Maybe she thought that she was still sleeping, because she couldn't accept what Nikki had just told her.

She sat up, and Nikki put her arm around her as she started to cry.

"He's dead, Mommy. J.R. is dead," Nikki cried, "and I can't believe this is happening."

Mother and daughter sat there crying together and holding each other. When they finally got up to go downstairs, Naomi told Nikki to go ahead and that she would be right behind her. As Nikki was going down the stairs, she heard a loud scream and rushed back to her mother's room. She found Naomi standing in the bathroom in front of the mirror.

"I'm all right. I just needed to get that out," Naomi told her daughter, and they went downstairs together.

Cairo and Butch had heard the scream and were waiting at the bottom of the stairs. They went into the living room and sat down.

"What happened?" Naomi asked once everybody was seated.

Cairo took a deep breath. "J.R. called me and said he needed me to ride with him to collect some money from Cromwell."

"Cromwell?" Nikki questioned. "I heard he left town."

"I heard that too."

"Was it Barlowe that sent him to collect from Cromwell?" Nikki asked him.

"I assumed it was either you or Barlowe."

"Wasn't me. Go on."

"So we ride out to Red Hook."

"Red Hook? Why the fuck would Cromwell wanna meet out there?" Nikki asked.

"I don't know, Nikki. I'm just telling you how it went down."

"I'm sorry, Cairo. Go on."

"It's cool. I understand." Cairo paused. "When we get out there, as soon as we got out of the car, they shot J.R. in the head."

"Red Hook. That's Garraway's turf," Butch said.

"That's what I'm saying. Why would Cromwell wanna meet out there?" Nikki asked again.

"I think it was a setup," Cairo said. "No. I'm sure it was a setup."

"No shit!" Nikki shouted. "But why?"

"You think it had something to do with us hitting their spot?" Butch asked.

"Could be," Nikki said and thought for a minute. "I knew when he told me about it that something was gonna come of it. Just not this."

Meanwhile, Remy was at his house. He had gotten the word that it was done, but Cairo had driven him to the hospital. Now, he was waiting for confirmation that J.R. was dead.

"Hello."

"We need to meet," Arya said.

"Altravessar. Thirty minutes."

When Arya arrived at Altravessar, Remy was already there. He was seated at a table in the rear of the club.

"I don't have much time. J.R. is dead."

"Good."

"Is there anything that can tie the shooter to you?"

"I used out-of-town shooters." Remy looked at his watch. "They're on a flight back to Chicago as we speak."

"Good. If anybody asks you anything about Cromwell, you say he reached out to you about getting right, and you told him he needed to talk to Barlowe, and he said he's been trying and can't get in touch with him."

"All right. What's your plan?"

"You let me worry about how to spin it. I gotta get back," Arya said and stood up. "We'll talk soon," she said and left Altravessar.

Arya needed to get back to the house to begin spinning that story for Barlowe, and she needed to do it before Nikki got there. However, when she arrived, Nikki was already there. She confronted Barlowe with the question.

"Why would Cromwell wanna meet in Red Hook?"

"I don't know, Nikki," Barlowe said. "Do you have any idea who did this, or what it's about? I'm thinking Garraway."

"I am, too," Nikki said as the library door burst open.

"I just heard," Arya said when she came sashaying into the room. "I am so sorry, Nikki."

"Thank you."

"You talked to Cromwell," Barlowe began, and it raised an eyebrow for Nikki. "What did he say?"

"I told you. He said he's been trying to get in touch with you so he can make things right. He said he had the money and wanted you to send somebody to meet him at the Red Hook Houses tonight at eight."

"And you're sure it was Cromwell?" Barlowe asked.

"I'm sure." Arya paused and looked at Nikki. "That drug murder in Red Hook a couple of weeks ago. Was that J.R.?"

"Yeah. What do you know about that?" Nikki asked.

Barlowe looked confused. "Wait. What drug murder in Red Hook?"

"You remember hearing about that drug murder in Red Hook on the news? That was J.R.," Arya informed him.

She knew that it was J.R. because she had Butch under her spell, and he gladly kept Arya informed of what was going on for the promise of sex one day.

"J.R. did that?" Barlowe asked.

"Yeah." Nikki nodded.

"The word is this was retaliation for the murders," Arya said to them.

"Yeah. Butch thinks the same thing," Nikki said and stood up.

"Where are you going?"

"I need some air," she said.

She walked out of the house, got in her car, and drove off. But Nikki didn't need air. She was mad, wanted revenge, and she had a plan. She drove straight to Marquee to see Chrystal. Nikki knew that she used to date a guy named Tyrone Wilkes, who was a major dealer for Garraway.

"What about him?"

"He's got a brother, doesn't he?"

"He does. Why?"

"What was his name?"

"Cedric. Why?"

"I need to find him. Tonight."

"I know he likes to hang out at a place called Burners. It's a little bar in Long Island City."

"Take me out there."

"Now?"

"Yes, now." Nikki started for the door. "Come on," she ordered, and Chrystal drove her to Burners.

Once they were there, Nikki and Chrystal went inside and looked around the small but crowded bar. Everybody was having a good time, minding their business. That was when they saw him.

"Leave," Nikki said.

"What?"

"Leave now. I'll be all right," Nikki said, keeping her eyes on Cedric Wilkes as he sat talking to a woman.

"You sure?"

"Yes, Chrystal, I'm sure. Now, get out of here."

"All right," Chrystal said, and she turned to leave.

Nikki watched her until she was out of the bar. Then, she took out her silenced gun and strolled toward the table where Cedric Wilkes was sitting. Without a word, Nikki put the barrel of her gun to his temple and pulled the trigger. His blood splattered on the face of the woman he was sitting with, and she screamed. Most of the other patrons didn't hear the shot over music. They were minding their business, having a fun time, and didn't see anything.

With the gun at her side, Nikki walked calmly out of Burners. She was walking down the street when a car pulled up alongside her.

"Get in!" Chrystal shouted.

Nikki got in the car. "I thought I told you to leave."

"You did. But you know I'm hardheaded and don't listen," Chrystal said as she drove Nikki away from there.

Chapter Twenty-two

His lips moved across her cheek and down her throat. Her head drifted back, and her eyes closed as he kissed her neck. His lips trailed a path down her chest to her breasts. He pressed them together with his hands, taking both nipples into his mouth. Arya cried out.

Remy worked her slowly and thoroughly. He pumped harder, his hand rubbing nipples, grabbing her breasts as they bounced. Their bodies contorted before falling back against the sheets.

"That was a long time coming," Arya said, breathing hard and smiling. She looked over at him, grinning.

"I've been wanting you for a long time," Remy said as he watched Arya get out of bed. He propped up a pillow and made himself comfortable.

J.R. was dead. Arya had made that possible. She had been flirting and teasing Remy for years. But Remy was smart enough to know that Arya didn't do it out of the kindness of her heart. For one, he didn't think Arya had a heart, and he had known her long enough to know that she did everything for a reason. That reason always benefited Arya.

She was fuckin' that nigga. And when she found out he was fuckin' Francine too, he had to die. I'm good with that, he thought.

That was fine by him, and to top it off, she finally brought him that pussy he'd been wanting, so it was all good. The only loose end was Francine. He hadn't seen her since she drove away from his house. He had his whole team looking for her, but nobody had seen her.

Remy didn't know how long she'd been standing there before she left, but she'd heard enough. If she told Nikki that he was in on the plan, she'd kill him. He needed to find Francine and make sure that didn't happen. J.R.'s funeral was the next day, and the last thing he needed would be for Francine to show up at her dead lover's funeral with a story to tell.

Since neither Nikki nor Naomi felt up to it, Megan had made all of the funeral arrangements for J.R. Mother and daughter had spent the days since his death at Naomi's house. Their days were filled with tears, good food from wherever they ordered, and plenty of reminiscing about the son and brother they'd lost. But that wasn't all Nikki was doing. Someone had killed her brother, and she was going to get revenge. Killing some random guy because he was somebody's brother wasn't enough. Not for Nikki. She needed to know who had ordered her brother killed and why.

Nikki didn't leave her mother's side, so Cairo and Butch were her eyes and ears in the streets. The second she heard that Arya had been involved in Barlowe sending J.R. to meet Cromwell, she became suspicious. Arya was the worst kind of snake. Everyone but Barlowe knew that. Or maybe he did, and that's why he kept her around. But it didn't matter to Nikki. Something didn't ring true about her story, so she had Cairo and Butch looking for Cromwell.

She had been avoiding talking to Barlowe. If her suspicions about Arya were correct, she needed to have her facts in place before she took them to him. There was also the possibility that he was involved, so Nikki decided to tread lightly for the time being. She would have her revenge when the time was right.

What she needed to know was about Garraway. She had heard the name Duncan Garraway all her life, but all she knew was that Garraway, her father, and Barlowe were friends, allies, but not much more than that. It was a subject neither her mother nor Barlowe wanted to talk about. All she knew for sure was that his organization was formidable. That didn't matter either. If Nikki found out he was involved, she would take apart that organization, piece by piece.

On the day of the service, family, friends, and associates gathered to pay their final respects to J.R. "We remember our loved one whose memory is a comforting embrace to us today. A life fulfilled, no longer caught up in the earthly struggle. Eternity is a restful place. Joy is theirs. We pray that until the day comes and we are joined in the great beyond, there will only be gladness in the memories we hold dear of this deserving soul. Good and wonderful God, we say goodbye to our departed loved one for one last time. We grieve because we will not see them any longer. But we also celebrate because we know that our loved one is enjoying your presence right now, without sickness or pain. We rejoice because we know that our loved one is safe and at peace. Please welcome your son Edward into glory, and free him from all physical frailties and all mental and emotional struggles. Thank you for this wonderful gift of eternal life. Amen."

After the service, Megan planned a celebration of life where there was plenty of food and drink, as well as the music from the mixes J.R. had made. Sharonda Braelin, J.R.'s girlfriend, sat with Nikki and Naomi. Some of his other women were there also. Although she had threatened to kill J.R. and he chased her away at gunpoint, Shekira attended the funeral and the celebration of life.

Nikki had noticed a couple of women that she knew J.R. was having sex with, but the one she didn't see was Francine. Remy was there, and the fact that Francine wasn't with him was noticeable. The other noticeable thing was that Arya was up in Remy's face.

What is up with that unholy alliance? Nikki asked herself.

She looked at Barlowe as he came toward her and wondered why he had put up with Arya. What was the hold that she had on him? Nikki shook her head because it didn't matter.

"How you doing?" Barlowe said, standing over Nikki.

Nikki looked up. "I'm fine."

"Can I sit?"

"Go ahead. Megan tells me you're paying for all this," Nikki said as he sat down. "Thank you. I appreciate it."

"It was the least I could do. Megan said that you and your mom were having a tough time dealing with it. So, this was one less thing to burden yourselves with."

"Thank you. I'm sure Mommy appreciates it too."

"You know, you and I need to talk."

"I know. But not here, not now."

"I get it, but we need to talk about what happened and what we're gonna do about it."

"I know, Uncle Pete. I just can't talk about it now. Not here. Tomorrow. I promise. Tomorrow, I'll come by the house, and we'll sit down and talk about it." Nikki stood up. "I'm gonna get the people that did this. I swear on my daddy's grave, everybody involved is gonna pay."

"See you tomorrow."

Chapter Twenty-three

As promised, Nikki planned to go to Barlowe's house the following day to talk. Since the shooting, Cairo and Butch had been very protective of Nikki. Therefore, despite her insistence that she'd be all right, they picked her up and drove her to Barlowe's house. She was glad that Arya was out shopping or doing whatever her snake ass did when they got there. Nikki didn't trust Arya, and her involvement in J.R.'s trip to Red Hook raised red flags. While Cairo and Butch waited in the living room, Nikki went to the library where Barlowe was waiting.

"How's it going, Nikki?"

"I'm getting better. But it's still hard."

"I know. I wish I could tell you that it's going to get better, but it doesn't. All I can tell you is that it gets easier with time."

"Thanks. That's good to know. Or at least it will be one day when it gets easier. But here and now, this shit hurts."

"I get it."

"What can you tell me about Garraway?"

"You planning on going after him?"

"If he's involved, fuck yeah, I'm going after him."

Barlowe nodded and sipped his drink. "Me, your father, Duncan Garraway, and Art Ward, we all used to work for Philip 'Lucky' Benjamin before we made the decision to take him out. He had been fighting a war with Thomas Robinson, and Ward saw an opportunity to switch allegiance. Ward makes a secret deal with Robinson to murder Benjamin in exchange for control of his rackets. Joe Bugs warned Benjamin about the murder plot. Benjamin was killed at a Coney Island restaurant. The gunmen were me, your father, Duncan Garraway, and Art Ward. Ward took over Benjamin's gang and became Robinson's lieutenant."

"What happened to Ward?"

"I'm getting to that." Barlowe got up and went to the bar. "You want a drink?"

"No, thank you."

"Robinson had a problem with three of his people—Hill, King, and Lee—and ordered us to take care of them. I escorted them into the club. Once the men were inside, Ward signaled the attack, and we started shooting. I remember seeing Ward shoot Lee in the head. When all three were dead, we left the building. I don't know why, but for some reason, Robinson was pissed that he shot him in the head.

"Over the next few months, Robinson had grown tired of Ward's constant complaints about Robinson's leadership. So, one day, Robinson gave the order—Art has got to go. So, the plan was for Eddie to invite Ward to a meeting to resolve a disagreement with a guy named Henderson about a marijuana racket. Robinson wanted Ward's murder to look like a drug deal gone wrong.

"Ward was to meet Robinson at a spot in Manhattan. When he got there, Garraway told Ward that they were driving to a different spot, and he picked up me and Eddie on the way. As Garraway drove the car, Eddie shot Ward to death with seven bullets. Then we drove to a deserted street in the Bronx to dump the body."

"Fascinating story. What happened to Robinson?"

"We knew eventually Robinson would turn on us the same way he had turned on Ward. He was going to a meeting at the 20/20 Club to work out a peace agreement with some of his rivals, but Robinson's real plan was to assassinate his adversary. We set up an ambush in the club storeroom, with the three of us wearing ski masks and hiding in a closet.

"When Robinson arrived at the 20/20 Club with his guys, he was escorted to the storeroom, and the three of us rushed out of the closet and started shooting. Eddie shot Robinson, knocking him to the floor. He got up and tried to run out of the room, but Eddie shot him in the back. Me and Garraway took out his men."

"So, Robinson's out of the way. What happened then?"

"After that, Garraway went off on his own." Barlowe shook his head. "We went round and round, fighting for turf until the three of us formed the Council to settle our disputes."

"What happened to the Council?"

"Garraway walked away after your father was murdered."

"You think he might have had something to do with Daddy's murder?"

"No. Garraway's good man. No, I don't think he did."

"So, tell me again, what happened with J.R.?"

"I sent J.R. to collect from Cromwell."

"Who nobody's seen or heard from in months. And you didn't think anything of that?"

"At the time, no, Nikki, I didn't."

"Cairo and Butch have been doing some checking, and they heard that Cromwell was an associate of Duncan Garraway back in the day, but he beat them out of some money too."

"Cromwell owed a lot of people a lot of money."

"That's why he got ghost. Then, out of the blue, he calls Arya, talking about getting right with you." Nikki shook her head.

"I'm sorry, Nikki. I should have talked to him myself, but I wasn't thinking."

"You mean you weren't thinking anything beyond getting your money."

"I'm sorry."

"Sorry ain't gonna bring J.R. back." Nikki glared at Barlowe. "But I get it."

"What you gonna do now?"

"What you think I'm gonna do? I'm going to find out if Garraway or any of his people had anything to do with J.R.'s murder, and I'm gonna kill them all. That's what I'm gonna do. What you gonna do?"

"I'm gonna help you get that done."

Nikki stood up. "Thanks, Uncle Pete."

Barlowe chuckled. "You only call me Uncle Pete when you want something."

"You're right. I want the people who did this to die. Slowly and painfully, if I can help it. That's what I want."

However, Nikki wasn't the only one plotting a path to revenge. Tyrone Wilkes, a major player in Garraway's organization, had buried his brother, Cedric, the day before. Several witnesses at Burners that night identified Nikki as the shooter. Wilkes had been checking with Cedric's people, trying to find a reason for the hit, but to a man, each of Cedric's people said he had no dealings with Nikki or anybody associated with Barlowe.

"I have no idea why she killed him," James Brooks, Wilkes's top lieutenant, said.

"Fuck it. Find Nikki Marx and kill her," were Wilkes's orders.

His people caught up with Nikki, Butch, and Cairo at a place called Mama's Uptown. They stuffed themselves on ribs, pulled pork, and greens. Nikki, on the other hand, hadn't had much of an appetite since J.R.'s murder. She ordered a half pint of shrimp mac and cheese, but she didn't finish that.

"What can you tell me about the spots Garraway's people run?"

"He's got four spots that they run the majority of his product out of. Those are the money makers," Cairo began, and he laid out their operation for Nikki. "That's the spot Tyrone Wilkes runs for him."

"Make that first on the list," Nikki ordered.

"What you got against Wilkes?"

"Nothing."

"Right," Butch said. "This is business."

"No. It's not business. This shit is very personal to me. I heard that this was retaliation for y'all hitting his spot."

"I've been hearing that, too," Butch said. All that meant was that Arya was doing a good job spreading the word.

"J.R. is dead, and everybody gotta pay for that."

"I heard you," Cairo said. He was still dealing with the fact that his best friend had died because he didn't get him to the hospital fast enough to save his life. "Let's kill them all. I don't give a fuck who, as long as they die for this," Cairo said to Nikki.

"Every last one."

Unbeknownst to them, Wilkes's people had set up an ambush outside of Mama's. When Cairo and Butch finished eating, Nikki paid the check and tipped their server, and they left Mama's. As soon as they stepped outside, Wilkes's men began shooting at them with AK-47s.

Nikki dove for the ground as the barrage of gunfire shattered the window behind her. She crawled to cover behind a car and took out her gun. She looked around for Cairo and Butch. Cairo had taken cover behind the car next to her, but she didn't see Butch.

"Butch!" she shouted.

"I'm all right!" he shouted back. He was able to make it to cover behind a truck in the parking lot. "Cover me!"

When Nikki and Cairo opened fire at the ambushers, Butch came running out from cover, blasting. He caught one on the shoulder as he ran, but it allowed Nikki to get a clean shot at one of the ambushers, and Cairo shot the other.

"You all right?" Nikki asked Butch as she emerged from cover. She looked at the wound.

"It's just scratch," Butch reported.

"Still, we need to get that taken care of. Let's go. I have a friend that's a nurse," Nikki said, and Cairo drove them to her friend Tasheka's house to tend to Butch's wound.

Chapter Twenty-four

When they got to Tasheka's apartment, she checked on Butch's gunshot wound. It was more than just a scratch. The bullet went through. She cleaned and dressed the wound.

"He just needs to rest," Tasheka told Nikki.

"Is it all right if he stays here for a while?"

"No problem. He can stay as long as he needs to."

"Thanks." Nikki stood up. "Let's go, Cairo."

"Where y'all going?" Butch asked.

"We're gonna hit the warehouse. They won't be expecting us to go right back at them," Nikki said, and Butch started to get out of bed.

"I'm going with you," Butch said.

"No. You got shot and probably lost a lot of blood. You need to rest," Tasheka said.

"I'll be fine." Butch got up and put his shirt on.

"Tell him he needs to rest, Nikki," Tasheka pleaded.

"Man says he's fine, then he's fine. Let's go do this," Nikki said and led her men out of Tasheka's apartment.

"You sure you up to this?" Nikki asked when they got in the car.

"I'm fine, Nikki. It was just a scratch."

"Okay, as long as you're good."

"I'm good," Butch said.

Cairo drove them out to one of Garraway's cook spots that was run by Treshawn and Beckham. As soon as they reached the structure and got to the stairs that led inside the warehouse, they went up carefully. Cairo kicked in the door, and Nikki went in firing. Once she made it inside and was set, she covered, while Cairo and Butch made it into the building.

Cairo stood up, firing, and Nikki had to dive on the floor as the men opened fire. Butch returned fire while lying on the ground. He made it to his feet, and they exchanged fire. The man ran down the hall, and Butch shot him as he ran.

Nikki moved down the hall, stopping in each room and firing at anybody she saw. Suddenly, a man came out of the closet when Nikki went into the room. The man fired once and missed. When Nikki raised her weapon to return fire, the man took cover. They exchanged gunfire. Nikki fired again and put him down with two to the chest.

While Cairo and Butch shot it out with Treshawn's men, Nikki approached the staircase and saw Beckham coming down. He fired a couple of shots at her and ran back up the steps. Nikki stopped at the bottom of the stairs, fired back, and then she went up after him. When she reached the top of the stairs, Beckham stopped, turned, and fired at Nikki. She stopped on the steps and fired back. Nikki made it to the top of the stairs, but she had to take cover immediately.

When Butch and Cairo reached the second level, they found Nikki pinned down and taking heavy fire. They fired a couple of shots at Beckham. It gave Nikki time to get to her feet. Beckham ran into a room. Nikki was about to go in after him, but Treshawn began firing wildly at her, and Nikki had to run for cover. Cairo fired at Treshawn to cover Nikki. When Treshawn turned to return fire at Cairo, Nikki stepped out and fired at him. She hit Treshawn with three shots, and he went down.

Nikki opened fire to give Cairo cover. He stayed low as he got to a better angle on the shooter. Cairo rose up and fired, taking him out with a shot in the chest. He kept firing wildly as he stumbled and fell over the rail. When he did, Nikki came out from cover and immediately had to retreat and run for cover as two more men with automatic weapons began firing at her. She dove to the floor and covered her head.

Butch aimed his weapon and opened fire, hitting one of the gunmen. That gave Nikki the time she needed to get to her feet and make it to better cover, as Cairo took down the other shooter. When Butch and Cairo returned fire, it sent the shooters rushing to take cover. Once they reached better cover, the two shooters sprayed the area with bullets.

Nikki dove for the ground and crawled along the floor to reach a spot where she could get to her feet. Cairo and Butch fired a couple of shots as they moved to better cover. With their gunfire focused on her men, Nikki was able to quietly move in behind one of the shooters. She put her gun to the base of his skull and pulled the trigger.

Cairo and Butch fired on the one remaining shooter. He kept firing until his weapon was empty, but before he could get to his handgun, Cairo took him down with one shot to the head. Nikki stood over him and put two in his chest.

"Everybody all right?" Nikki asked once the shooting ended.

"I'm good," Butch said, but he was holding his shoulder.

"I'm all right."

"Gather up the dope and the paper, and let's get outta here," Nikki ordered, and they got to their work.

After completing their task, the three went to Club XL to regroup. They sat in the packed club, planning their next move.

"What y'all getting ready to do?" Nikki asked.

"Gotta pick up some money from Goodell," Cairo said.

"Y'all don't need me for that, do you?" Nikki asked.

"Naw. Just picking up some paper," Butch assured her.

"Good. Then I'm gonna sit this one out," Nikki informed them.

"Okay. We'll take you home, and then we'll go," Cairo suggested.

"No. I need to talk to Sierra before I go. Y'all go ahead."

"You gonna be all right?" Cairo asked.

"Yes, Cairo, I'll be fine. I'll have a couple of Sierra's people walk me to my car, and we got people at my mother's house."

"You sure?" Butch asked.

"Yes, I'm sure. Y'all go handle your business, and I'll get with you tomorrow."

Cairo stood up. "Okay. But you need to call me when you get to the house."

"I promise I will. Now, go."

Nikki watched Cairo and Butch until they had pulled their way out of a packed Club XL before she got up and made her way, as quickly as she could, to the office to talk to Sierra.

"Damn!" Nikki said aloud. "There's a lot of paper in this bitch today."

However, when she got to the office, there was no sign of Sierra. For the next fifteen minutes, Nikki wandered around the club and finally found Sierra in the gambling room. She was settling a dispute between two players who each had accused the other of cheating. Guns were drawn, and Sierra was in the middle of it.

Nikki took out her gun and watched as Sierra talked the men down, and each of them lowered their weapons. She tried to get them to shake hands, but that was a bridge too far for both of them.

"Can I see you in your office when you get done here?" Nikki said, putting away her gun and walking away.

When Sierra got to the office twenty minutes later, Nikki was waiting behind her desk. She plopped down in one of the chairs in front of the desk.

"What a night," Sierra said and exhaled.

"Looked like. Everything taken care of?"

"It certainly is. I thought they were going to kill each other for a second there," Sierra said.

"But you handled it." Nikki slapped her hands. "Take a bow."

"Thank you. Thank you," Sierra said, bowing in her seat.

"I wanted to ask you how it was going, being manager and all, but I see you got it handled."

"You know this is my spot. Of the three clubs you own, this has always been my favorite. So, I was super excited when you gave me the job. But I gotta tell you, Nikki, I was scared to death that first couple of days." Sierra laughed. "A couple of weeks ago, I was a display model for a cosmetics company, and now I'm running a nightclub—and a gambling club. But I was surprised at how much I knew just from being here all the time."

"Being a club rat finally paid off."

"Despite what my mother said." Sierra giggled. "I gotta be honest with you, I have never worked this hard on any job ever, but I am having the time of my life. So, thank you."

"I knew you could handle it." Nikki laughed. "You're too smart to be doing a Vanna White impersonation for the rest of your life."

"Tell me about it."

Nikki stood up. "I'm about to get outta here. Have a couple of security guys meet me at the door."

"If you don't mind me asking, what do you need them for?" Sierra asked.

"To walk me to my car, Sierra." She shook her head. "What did you think? I was recruiting them for some wet work?"

"Word is you're taking us to war, so I just thought I'd ask," Sierra said, picking up the phone to make the request.

"Good night, Sierra. I'll talk to you tomorrow," Nikki said, leaving the office and heading to the front door. Two members of security were waiting when she got there.

"How y'all doing?"

"What's up, boss?"

"What's up, Nikki? Reporting for escort duty."

"Let's go."

On the way out of XL, Nikki saw Shekira at the bar. She had tried to kill J.R., and it made Nikki wonder if she knew anything about him getting killed. She thought for a second about going over there and asking her, but Nikki decided the possibility of that was slim.

That was about that dick, Nikki thought and kept making her way toward the door.

Once they got outside of the club and walked toward her car, a car came speeding down the street with its bright lights on.

"Get down!" one of the security guards yelled and dove in front of Nikki. He took her to the ground, taking a bullet to the stomach in the process.

When the shooting stopped, the car drove off. The guard began firing as the vehicle sped away. He hit one of the tires, and the car crashed.

"You all right?" Nikki asked her fallen soldier.

"I'll be all right," he said, holding his stomach.

Nikki got up, got her gun out, and ran toward the car, along with security. When they reached the car, both the driver and the shooter were dazed. Nikki shot them both.

"Call the chop, have them come get this car, and then take care of the body," Nikki ordered.

"On it."

Nikki quickly walked to the car and looked at the dead bodies of her attackers. Never having seen either of them before, she went to check on her fallen soldier.

Chapter Twenty-five

Rah-Rah called Cairo, but once again, he didn't answer. She looked at Bey. Rah-Rah had met him the night before at a party that one of Thatcher's friends was having. They met, hung out, laughed, drank, and had a good time, but when Bey said he had a little package and wanted to go somewhere and party, Rah-Rah went to his apartment in Queens.

When they got to his apartment, Rah-Rah danced while he cooked. Then they smoked all he had and then called his connect, Jaylynn, for more. Both Rah-Rah and Bey were restless and a little horny, and she liked him, so they had sex to pass to time while they waited for someone to bring them some more to smoke.

When Jaylynn arrived early that morning, he saw Rah-Rah and decided to smoke with them. The three spent the morning in the bathroom, smoking until they had finished just about all that he had with him. At that point, Bey went into the bedroom to lie down, encouraging Rah-Rah to come with him because he wanted to have sex.

"I'm coming," she said, but she didn't move. The only thing on her mind was getting another hit. Rah-Rah sat there patiently while Jaylynn cleaned the residue from the pipe. When he was finished cleaning the pipe, they smoked the residue. When that was done, he looked at Rah-Rah.

And smiled.

"Check this out. I'm gonna go get us another little taste."

"Cool."

He shut the door and reached into his pocket. "You let me fuck you, and I got a gram I can cook up for you," he said, holding up the bag.

Rah-Rah took the bag from his hand, and without saying a word, she just stood up, took off her pants, and bent over the sink. As quickly as he could, Jaylynn pulled down his pants, stroked his dick a few times, and went up in her. Rah-Rah stared emotionlessly at her reflection in the mirror while Jaylnn pounded away.

She was letting another man fuck her, so she should keep getting high. At least she liked Bey; she didn't even know Jaylynn, and on top of that, he was ugly. But there he was, balls deep inside her. She wondered how she had allowed this to happen to her, but all the while, she was hoping Jaylynn would be quick.

When he was done, Jaylynn was as good as his word. He cooked up what he had, and then Rah-Rah went with him to get more. Once they returned to Bey's apartment, the three spent the afternoon once again smoking up everything Jaylynn had come back with.

"I'm done fuckin' with you two. Bey, I'll get with you tomorrow," Jaylynn said, and he left.

That was hours ago. Since then, Bey had been calling around, trying to get somebody to bring them some more to smoke, but neither he nor Rah-Rah had any money, so that wasn't happening.

She decided to try Cairo again.

"What's up, Rah?" Cairo answered.

"I need a favor."

"Yeah, what's that?"

"I need a little something, but I don't have any money. Can you help a sister out?"

"Yeah, Rah. I got you. I'm in the middle of something right now, but you can come by the crib later and I got you."

"That's cool. I'm out in Queens, so it's gonna take me a minute to get there."

"I'll call you when I'm on my way home." Cairo ended the call. He glanced over at Butch as he drove. "I'ma fuck Rah-Rah's muthafuckin' ass tonight."

"Soon as we take care of this business, you can fuck the shit outta her," Butch said and pulled over in front of an abandoned gas station. There were two cars parked outside.

"I thought you told Morgan to come alone," Cairo said.

"I thought that too. Some niggas just don't listen."

Butch and Cairo checked their weapons before they got out of the car and approached the building. As they got closer, the garage door opened.

"Come on in," Kurtis, Morgan's right-hand man, said as he waved them in.

"I got a bad feeling about this," Cairo said as they went inside and Kurtis closed the garage door. Inside, another man was leaning against a car.

"Where's Morgan?" Butch asked, looking around.

"Morgan?" Kurtis chuckled. "He ain't here."

"Where's he at?" Butch asked.

"There's been a change in plans," Kurtis said.

"Gun!" Cairo yelled when he saw a third man with a gun in the shadows. The man began shooting as Cairo and Butch ran for cover.

Butch hit the floor and fired at Kurtis. He shot him in the back as he turned to run for cover. Cairo hit the one by the car with two shots to the chest. The third man stuck his head out and began firing. Cairo and Butch returned fire. He came running out, fired a couple of shots at them, and ran. Cairo reloaded his weapon and was about to go after him, but he didn't see that another man had come out the door and prepared to fire.

"Behind you, Cairo!" Butch yelled and took aim.

Cairo turned in time to see Butch drop him with a shot to the head before he went after the one that got away. That man ran out the back door, firing shots the entire way, then reloading his weapon on the run. He fired a few shots at Cairo and Butch, who were coming fast and firing at him. When he turned to fire, Cairo and Butch lit him up.

They walked over and stood over the body. Each shot him once more before they went back to the garage to look for the money that Morgan had told them to come pick up. They didn't find any money, but they did find Morgan. He was dead, shot execution style: on his knees, hands tied behind his back, and shot in the back of the head.

"Damn. That's fucked up," Butch said.

"Fucked up for him."

"Fucked up ain't no money here," Butch said, and they left to the sound of police sirens in the distance.

"What's up, Cairo?" Rah-Rah answered.

"I'm on my way home. Come on through."

"I'll be there in ten minutes," Rah-Rah said, ending the call and driving faster.

When Cairo and Butch arrived at their apartment, Butch said that he was tired and went to bed. Cairo straightened up the apartment a little before Rah-Rah got there. It was after two in the morning when Rah-Rah rang the bell.

"Sup, Rah," Cairo said when he opened the door.

"Hey, Cairo."

"Come in and make yourself comfortable," he said, stepping aside to allow Rah-Rah to come in. She came sauntering in. "You look nice."

"Thank you," she said and swung her hips a little harder for Cairo.

She was wearing the same black Cinq à Sept Giles Twill cargo jogger that she'd had on for the last two days, and she hadn't bathed. But Cairo didn't seem to care because Rah-Rah was fine, and he wanted to fuck her. He had wanted to for a long time, and now she was in his apartment.

"So, what can you do for me?" Rah-Rah asked, kicking out of her shoes and tossing her purse on the couch. She followed Cairo into the kitchen, where he handed her a small bag of rock.

"You learn how to cook yet?"

"No," she said, going back to the couch to get her purse.

"You get started on that," Cairo said and prepared to cook some cocaine for Rah-Rah to smoke.

Rah-Rah took the pipe and a lighter from her purse and returned to the kitchen. She sat down at the table, put a rock in the bowl, and lit up.

"Here you go," Cairo said, setting a plate with rocks on the table in front of Rah-Rah. Once she let the pipe cool, she put a big piece in the bowl.

"You not smoking?" she asked.

"Nope. But you go ahead and enjoy yourself," he said and went into the living room.

Cairo picked up his gaming remote to play Doom Eternal, one of the hottest games out. He assumed the role of Doom Slayer to protect the Earth and went into battle against the demon spawn.

The sun was just about to break the morning sky when Rah-Rah put the pipe down. She got up from the table and went into the living room. Cairo was gone. She went to the bedroom and looked in. When she saw Butch sleeping, she closed the door and went to the next room.

Cairo was in bed asleep when Rah-Rah came into his room. "Cairo," she called to him, but he didn't move.

Rah-Rah walked over to the bed, pulled back the covers, and saw that Cairo was sleeping naked. She pulled the cover back a little farther. "And you got a fat, juicy dick too."

She lay down on the bed next to Cairo and shook him. "Cairo."

"What's up?"

"You got any more?"

He opened one eye and looked at Rah-Rah, who was lying on the bed, leaning on her elbow with her breasts spilling out of her jogger top.

"Take off your clothes."

When he saw that Rah-Rah had gotten up and was taking off her clothes, Cairo sat up and pulled back the covers. He started stroking his dick while Rah-Rah got undressed.

"You are sexy as hell. I've been wanting to get with you since the first time I saw you."

"I've been checking you out for a minute, too." Rah-Rah crawled up on the bed and quickly took Cairo's dick to the back of her throat.

Rah-Rah teased his head with her tongue, and then she slowly worked her way down his shaft. She slid her soft, wet lips and tongue up and down his length, and then she relaxed the muscles in her throat and used the roof of her mouth to apply a little pressure on his shaft.

"Damn, Rah-Rah!"

She straddled his body and lowered herself onto him. Rah-Rah rode him slowly at first, and then she began to move her hips back and forth.

***

When Butch woke up, he sat up in bed and stretched. After a good yawn, he got out of bed, thinking that his shoulder felt better. He was glad he had gotten some rest, but he was hungry, and there was never any food in the apartment. Butch got dressed and came out of his room. He knocked on Cairo's door.

"What?" Cairo shouted as he arched his back and began pumping his dick into Rah-Rah as deep and as hard as he could.

"I'm going to get something to eat. You want something?"

"Yeah! Bring two of whatever you get yourself!" he shouted as Rah-Rah put her hands on his legs, her feet on the bed, and she bounced up and down on him.

"You got company?"

"Yeah!"

"Rah-Rah still here?"

"Yeah!"

"Hey, Rah-Rah," Butch said and peeped into the room to watch. "I'll be back," he said and closed the door.

When Butch came back, Cairo was back in the living room, back on the couch, playing Doom Eternal. Butch handed him his food.

"Rah-Rah still here?"

"She's in the room."

Butch got the food that he brought for her and went toward Cairo's room.

"Don't fuck her in my bed!" Cairo shouted as Butch went in.

A few minutes later, Cairo's bedroom door opened. Butch came rushing out, leading a naked Rah-Rah to his room and slamming the door.

Cairo smiled. "Yeah, we're keeping her."

Chapter Twenty-six

After visiting eleven ports of call aboard the Norwegian Prima, Duncan Garraway returned to New York from the fifteen-day Caribbean cruise he took with his new girlfriend, Capria Reynolds. She was thirty years younger than him, and they admittedly had little in common due to the age difference. However, they thoroughly enjoyed one another's company, and these last fifteen days confirmed what he had been thinking.

Garraway had never been married, never had found the so-called one. He'd had six children by six different women. Garraway was a good absentee father, as absentee fathers go. He took care of his children, and their mothers never wanted for anything. He got along with all of them, but relationships were never his thing.

It was different with Capria. He couldn't quite put his finger on why, but he was enjoying being with her more than he had any woman in the past. He thought that he might grow tired of her, having to spend fifteen days together, but he didn't. The time was wonderful, but now it was time to get back to business.

He glanced over at her, sitting next to him in the limousine, before taking out his phone and turning it on. It began ringing right away.

"And so it begins," Capria said, patting his hand.

"Hello."

"Good. You answered," Marques Jorell, Garraway's right-hand man and adviser, said.

"I just turned on the phone, and here you are."

"You on your way here?"

"I am. In the limo."

"Good. I'll see you when you get here. We got . . . issues."

Garraway chuckled. "Issues? I don't like the sound of that."

"Would you rather I said we got a lotta shit going on we gotta deal with?"

"No. I'd much rather hear everything was quiet and peaceful while you were gone, Dee. You could have gone on another cruise."

Marques laughed. "I wish I could see some shit like that, but I can't. So, I'll see you when you get here."

Garraway ended the call and looked at Capria. "Do you remember when we were in Willemstad, Curaçao, at Kenepa Beach, and you were saying how beautiful it was there?"

"And you said we should never leave. But we got back on the boat anyway. I remember." She squeezed his hand.

"Keep that thought in mind."

"Is it too soon to start planning our next trip?"

"It certainly isn't. You wanna take another cruise?"

"I don't know—maybe."

"If we did, I wanna take a European cruise."

"That might be cool. Start making it happen."

"Really?" Capria questioned excitedly.

"Yeah, why not?" Garraway leaned over and kissed Capria on the cheek.

He had reached a point in his life where he had everything he ever wanted or needed, and the game no longer posed a challenge as it had in his youth. Enjoying life and all it had to offer had become more important lately. Garraway looked at Capria and once again thought about walking away from it all.

Maybe it's time, Garraway thought as they made the drive to Cecilia Drive in Syosset.

The limousine pulled into the driveway in front of the five-bedroom house that had a fireplace and floor-to-ceiling windows in the living room, a beautiful gourmet chef's kitchen, and a home theatre room. One of the five bedrooms had been converted into a game room and home gym. The property also had a heated in-ground pool.

The driver got out. "Too late to turn back now," Garraway said.

"No, it's not. We can go right back to the port and get on whatever cruise is leaving next."

"That's a thought." The driver opened the door. "Let me see what issues Marques has for me, and then we'll see."

"I'm going to hold you to that," Capria said as Garraway got out of the limousine. He extended his hand for Capria, and she got out.

"I'm serious. Unless Marques tells me we're at war or something like that, you and I are going on another cruise," Garraway said, taking her in his arms and kissing her. Then he walked hand in hand with Capria into the house.

Marques Jorell was standing in the foyer when they came through the door.

"Hi, Marques," Capria said.

"Couldn't even let us get in the house good?" Garraway said.

"Hello, Capria."

She gave him a polite, sisterly kind of hug.

"How was your trip?"

"We had an amazing time. Tortola, in the British Virgin Islands, was beautiful, and I really liked Oranjestad, Aruba." She started up the stairs. "I'll show you the pictures if you wanna see them."

"Can't wait," he said, watching Capria until she was out of sight.

"Really? You can't wait to see our vacation pictures?" Garraway said.

"Gonna be the highlight of my day," Jorell said and followed Garraway into the game room where he liked to do business.

"So, what's going on that got you meeting me at the door?"

"We have a problem, and her name is Nikki Marx."

The mention of the name brought back memories of his friend Eddie. "Nikki? How is Nikki Marx a problem?"

"She's been going hard at Tyrone Wilkes for a week now."

"What's that about?"

"Somebody killed J.R."

"J.R. is dead?"

Garraway knew that Naomi must be taking it badly. Garraway thought about calling her, but they hadn't spoken since Eddie was murdered. Although she didn't believe he was involved, Naomi was angry because Garraway seemed unwilling to do anything about it.

"Somebody shot him at Red Hook. Since then, she's been at Wilkes. She killed his brother, Cedric, and then she robbed his cook spot."

"I don't understand why Pete would break the peace that's existed for years."

"They're not going all out against us. It seems like it's just Nikki, and it's about J.R."

"I need to talk to Pete."

"He called when it first jumped off. I told him you were out of the country and couldn't be reached."

Garraway nodded. "Okay. I need to talk to Wilkes."

"He's here in the living room."

"You thought of everything."

"I want to get past this as soon as possible." Jorell chuckled. "Honestly, Wilkes is getting on my nerves."

"Okay, Marques. Bring him in," Garraway said, and Jorell left the game room to go get Wilkes.

Garraway went behind the bar, got the landline phone, and set it on the bar. It had been years since he had spoken to Pete Barlowe, and changing that hadn't been on his mind when he woke up that morning. Since it had been years, Garraway wondered if his number was still the same.

He picked up the phone and was about to dial when Jorell came back into the room with Wilkes.

"Good evening, Mr. Garraway," Wilkes said respectfully.

"Tyrone. How are you?"

"I'm good, sir."

"Marques told me about your brother, Cedric. I am sorry for your loss."

"Thank you, Mr. Garraway."

Garraway came from behind the bar and stood in front of Wilkes. "Nikki Marx. What's going on with you two?"

"She thinks that I had something to do with her brother getting killed."

"Did you?"

"Sir?"

Garraway looked frustrated. "Did you have anything to do with her brother J.R. getting killed?"

"No, sir." Wilkes raised his right hand. "I didn't have anything to do with it."

Garraway shook his head and glanced at Jorell. "How did J.R. meet his maker?"

"He was in Red Hook, and somebody shot him in the head," Jorell answered.

"Funeral?"

"Closed casket."

"Yeah, she's pissed," he said, thinking about Naomi. He turned back to Wilkes, who was literally standing at attention. "What have you done?"

"Sir?"

Jorell and Garraway glanced at one another. "You said you didn't kill her brother. What have you done?"

"I tried to hit her outside Marquee, but she got away," Wilkes said. "Other than that . . ." He looked at Jorell. "I haven't done anything."

"Why is that? She killed your brother, and Marques tells me she robbed your cook house. And you haven't done anything. Why is that?"

"Mr. Jorell told me that we got some kind of arrangement with her people."

"Good man. At least you know how to follow orders," Garraway said.

Even if you ain't the brightest bulb in the bunch.

"Thank you, sir."

"What would you like to do now?"

"I would like for you to take these handcuffs off."

"Okay." Garraway walked away. "Thank you for speaking to me. I will let you know what I want done."

"But—" Wilkes began.

"He will let you know what he decides," Jorell said and extended his hand toward the door. Wilkes dropped his head and left the room.

"You say Pete ain't going all out on this?" Garraway asked.

"Nope." Jorell went to the bar and poured a drink. He held up the bottle. "You want one?"

"No. We did enough drinking on that ship to keep us drunk for another week. I need a day to dry out. But you say it's just Nikki?"

"Seems that way to me."

"And you've been doing this long enough to know."

Jorell had worked for Garraway for the last twenty years.

"You calling me old?"

"Yes. But old has its advantages. And, yes, I am talking about Wilkes."

"He's a little slow-thinking sometimes, but he's a good soldier, and he follows orders."

"It's the slow-thinking thing that concerns me." Garraway stood next to him at the bar. "The handcuffs are off. You have my blessing to handle this any way you see fit. You see fit, not Wilkes. I get the feeling he won't make the best decision on how to retaliate without drawing us into something that Pete will have to do something about. I am in no mood to fight a war with Pete Barlowe."

"Neither am I." Jorell chuckled. "That old shit you mentioned."

"Tell me about it. The handcuffs are off, but you make sure this kid understands our arrangement with Pete, and breaking it doesn't come easily. Therefore, he needs to follow your orders without deviation."

"You want me to take care of it myself?"

"No, you let the kid have his revenge. You just make sure it doesn't spill over into something bigger."

"You got it," Jorell said and finished his drink. "I'll let you know before it goes down."

"Do that," Garraway said as he watched Jorell leave the game room.

Chapter Twenty-seven

"It's going down tonight," Jorell reported.

"Let me know how it goes," Garraway said and ended the call.

Jorell put down the phone and looked at Wilkes. "Go ahead."

"Thank you, Mr. Jorell. I won't disappoint you."

"I know."

That night, Nikki, Cairo, and Butch were sitting at a table in the back of the Palace. Internationally known recording artist Salomé Warner was on stage performing, and they were discussing who they were going to hit next.

Wilkes left Jorell's office at Boom on East 48th and headed for the Palace. He had his people sitting on all three of Nikki's spots, waiting for her to show up at one of them. When Wilkes got the word that she, Cairo, and Butch were there, he informed Jorell and got his approval to proceed. Now that he had the go-ahead, he called his robbing team.

"We're on," Wilkes said and drove to the Palace.

The plan was to rob the front door and the gambling room and kill Nikki in the process. That was Jorell's plan, but it wasn't good enough for Wilkes. That plan was designed to maintain the peace that Jorell spent too much time explaining.

Especially since I didn't care, Wilkes thought.

Killing Nikki was his priority. He instructed his robbing team to follow Jorell's instructions to the letter. Get the money, kill Nikki, and get out. He had a plan of his own. When he got to the Palace, he called his men.

"Everybody is in position."

"Do it," Wilkes commanded.

Five of Wilkes's men came in the front door armed with mini-14s and began firing wildly around the club. One of the first shots hit Salomé Warner, and she went down. As one of the band members dragged her off stage, Nikki ran to the bar for cover, firing shots along the way. Cairo and Butch were right behind her. Cairo dove over the bar and came up shooting. He shot one of the attackers as Butch and Nikki made it behind the bar for cover.

There was chaos as some customers ran for the nearest exit, while others sought cover wherever they could find it. Several weren't that lucky. As they fired, Nikki crawled out from the bar and flipped over a table. She fired at the shooters, and they returned her fire. Nikki fired at one of the shooters and hit him with three shots, and he fell over, firing wildly.

While two other gunmen closed in on the bar and continued firing with AR15s, Butch returned their fire and ran out from behind the bar. The two men kept firing as Butch ran for better cover to reload.

While Butch made his way to better cover, two men came into the club. They had taken the money from the front door and were on their way to take the gambling room, while the other men exchanged gunfire with Nikki, Cairo, and Butch. The two men blanketed the club with bullets as they walked. One fired and hit a member of the Palace's security team with a shot to the chest before he could get a shot off. He went down. When he was close enough, the gunman shot and killed him as he passed.

Nikki stayed put behind the table until the shooting stopped. She got up while the shooters at the bar stopped to reload, then fired and hit one of them with three shots. The other turned quickly and fired at Nikki as she ran. Cairo then came up firing on the gunmen from behind the bar. One of his shots grazed the side of the man's head, and it disoriented him long enough for Cairo to put two in his chest. Cairo took the mini and two magazines from the one he had just killed and headed toward Nikki.

She saw the two gunmen heading for the gambling room and ran behind them. When she hit the door, the men were in the count room. One was holding his weapon to the head of the cashier while she put the money in a bag. The other covered.

Nikki saw Megan hiding behind the table with the roulette wheel. She took another look at the gunmen and made her way to Megan.

"You all right?"

"I'll be all right," she said, and Nikki handed Megan one of her guns. Megan put one in the chamber.

"Let's go," Nikki said to Megan, and they came up firing as the men came out of the count room.

The men shot back. Megan wasn't a good shot, but she emptied the magazine on the clip. She didn't hit anybody. Nikki fired twice, hitting him with one to the chest and one to the head. The other gunman picked up the bag of money and kept shooting as he made his way to the door. Nikki kept firing at him until he was out the door.

"Go!" Megan yelled at Nikki, and she went after him.

When the man came out of the gambling room, Butch and Cairo were still shooting it out with Wilkes's men.

"Let's go!" he shouted and began making his way, firing, to the exit. The other two shooters began backing their way toward the door. One fired at Cairo and missed.

As Nikki came running out of the gambling room, Cairo raised his weapon, fired, and hit a gunman with several shots to the chest. He fell over a table. Butch and Nikki were getting close to the shooters. Butch laid down cover fire, while Nikki moved closer. Once she made it and was set, she covered while Butch ran toward her position. When he made it to her, they both opened fire and fired at the last of the shooters, but the shooters made it out of the club.

The men ran to a van and got in. When Nikki and Butch came out of the Palace, they fired at the van as it drove away.

"Fuck!" Nikki shouted as she watched the taillights disappear from sight. Cairo joined them. "Go see how many people are hurt."

"On it," Butch said, and he and Cairo went back inside the Palace to carry out her orders.

Wilkes sat in his car, watching them until they were inside, and then he started the car. With the shooting inside over, customers began coming out of the Palace and rushing to their cars to get out of there.

As cars rolled out of the parking lot past Nikki, she didn't notice that Wilkes had rolled up alongside her. He rolled down the window.

"Hey, Nikki." He raised his weapon. "This is for Cedric."

Nikki dove for the ground as Wilkes fired. He drove off, and Nikki fired at the car as it sped out of the parking lot.

As he dove away from the Palace, Wilkes cursed himself for his arrogance. He had her, and all he had to do was pull the trigger. "But instead, you had to announce that shit like it was some fuckin' movie. Smart."

Butch and Cairo came running out of the Palace when they heard the shooting. They saw Nikki getting up from the ground.

"You all right?" Butch asked.

"Yeah, I'm okay."

"What happened?" Cairo asked.

"It was Wilkes. He caught my daydreaming, and I let him roll right up on me."

"He's stepping it up," Cairo said.

"We hit his main money spot tomorrow."

Chapter Twenty-eight

"Internationally known recording artist Salomé Warner and four others were victims of gunshot wounds when a shooting erupted while she was performing at the Palace nightclub. The victims were taken to New York Presbyterian Hospital to be treated. Ms. Warner, who suffered a gunshot to her left arm, was treated and released. For more on the shooting, we go live with our own Yolanda Teagen outside the Palace."

Jorell grabbed the remote and turned off the television. He got his keys and was about to leave when the phone rang. He glanced at the display and answered.

"Hello."

"You see the news?" Garraway asked.

"Yeah. I'm going to deal with it right now."

"I told you that this would happen."

"I know. I'm in damage control mode."

"Then control this. And, Marques, do it fast. Singers getting shot during what was supposed to be a robbery is not good. Maybe think about hiring out-of-town shooters that can hit what they're aiming at," Garraway said, and he ended the call.

Jorell left the house and drove to the place where he knew Wilkes would be. And sure enough, there he was, sitting on the hood of a car that was parked outside his trap house. Wilkes controlled the traffic and the business conducted in the courtyard and selected apartments throughout the building.

When Wilkes saw Jorell's car, he jumped down from the hood of the vehicle. He exhaled because he wasn't looking forward to this and hoped that he wouldn't have to die for it. It would have been better for him if he had actually killed Nikki. At least he would have that to show for his efforts. But all he had was money, dead soldiers and civilians, and Salomé Warner in the hospital.

Jorell rolled down the window when Wilkes got to the car. "Get in."

Wilkes looked in the back seat before he got in the car. "What the fuck happened?"

"Collateral damage."

"Collateral damage my ass, nigga. Fuckin' Salomé Warner in the hospital is you fuckin' up, not some fuckin' collateral damage."

"I'm sorry."

"Damn right, you're sorry. Get the money, and get Nikki in the process. It was a simple plan, and you fucked it up." Jorell shook his head. "Where's the rest of your team?"

"They are all dead."

"At least you got one thing right."

"With Salomé Warner getting shot, I knew I had to. He said his man was shooting wild in the air to scatter the crowd, and one of the shots hit Warner."

"Good explanation. But, one, I don't give a fuck, and two, Warner is still in the hospital because you fucked up."

"I shot him in the head anyway."

"Where's the money?"

"In my car."

"Go get it."

"All of it?"

"Yeah, nigga, all of it. Fuck-ups ain't free."

Wilkes sat looking angrily at Jorell.

"What are you waiting for? Go get the money?"

"Yes, Mr. Jorell," Wilkes said and got out of the car.

It was ten minutes later when Wilkes returned to Jorell's car with the bag of money.

"Toss it in the backseat," Jorell ordered.

Wilkes threw the bag with the money in the back seat and leaned in through the window.

"I suggest you lay low for a while." He started the car. "I saw Nikki on the news. She looked pissed."

Jorell rolled up the window and drove off, knowing that if Nikki didn't kill him, he would have Wilkes dead before the week was out.

Fuck-ups ain't free.

As Jorell was driving away from Wilkes's spot, Nikki was on her way there with Butch and Cairo. That morning, when she woke up, Nikki had breakfast with her mother, and then she went to talk to Barlowe. Nikki was surprised and happy when she arrived and found out that Arya was gone. Conversations with Barlowe always went better when she wasn't around.

When Nikki got there, Barlowe was in his kitchen having waffles and sausage for breakfast.

"Sorry to interrupt your meal," Nikki said when she came into the room.

"That's okay. Come in and sit down."

Nikki glanced at the television on the counter. The news of Salomé Warner's shooting was on the news.

"You hungry?"

"No. I had breakfast with Mommy."

He picked up the remote and turned off the television.

"You talk to Queen?" Nikki asked.

"Yeah, I talked to her. Queen was not happy about her girl getting shot in my club."

"What does she want?"

"You mean other than me covering all of her medical bills?"

"Yeah, other than that."

"She wants to sit down and discuss it." Barlowe pointed his fork at Nikki. "I don't need this shit right now, Nikki."

"I know that you don't. You think I do?"

"You wanna tell me what happened?"

"It was a hit designed to look like a robbery. One team took the front door and the gambling room, and the other came after me, Cairo, and Butch."

"You know who it was?"

Nikki nodded. "It was Wilkes. He took a shot at me in the parking lot when the shooting was over inside."

Barlowe chuckled. "How'd you let that happen?"

"We ran out after the robbers. I just wasn't expecting him. But he rolled right up on me. If the fool had just shot me instead of letting me know he was there, I'd be dead now."

"Glad it didn't come to that."

"Me too."

"You got an end game in mind?" Barlowe asked.

"Yeah. I'm gonna kill Wilkes. That's my end game."

"I tried to reach out to Duncan Garraway, but his gorilla said he was out of the country and couldn't be reached."

"You believe him?"

" Jorell's a lot of things, but he's got no reason to lie to me. Not about that anyway. I'll reach out to him again."

"What you gonna tell him? That Eddie Marx's little girl went rogue and can't be controlled?"

"Can you?"

"Can I what? Be controlled?"

"Yes. Can you be controlled?"

"I'm not out of control now. Am I?"

"No. You're not."

"Anytime you think I am out of control, pull me back. Being out of control is bad for your health and for business."

"That proves that you're not out of control."

"I'm on top of this, Uncle Pete. I told you that you could trust me, and you can. I just need to finish this business and find out what really happened with J.R."

"Ain't that what this thing with Wilkes is about?"

"Maybe. Maybe not. The whole shit with Cromwell showing back up outta nowhere bothers me."

"You mean you don't trust Arya."

"No. I don't. I know that's your woman, but if her lips are moving, she's telling a lie. Everybody sees that but you."

Barlowe looked away. "Arya serves a purpose."

"And on that note,"—Nikki stood up—"I'm gone."

That was earlier in the day. Since then, Nikki had spent the day hunting down Wilkes to kill him. Her sources told her that, as she suspected, he was at his main spot. It made sense that he would be there. He damn near had an army spread throughout that building, so it was where Wilkes was best protected. They would have to count on the element of surprise. Hit the spot and get out quick.

When they got there, there were four men in the courtyard doing business. She didn't see Wilkes in his usual spot. Cairo brought the car to a stop, and Nikki jumped out of the vehicle with two weapons blasting. Guns were pulled, and they were immediately fired on.

Cairo and Butch fired and hit their targets with shots to the head and chest. Two men drew their weapons and opened fire blindly as they ran toward the street. They were met by Nikki, who killed them as they ran.

When the other two opened fire, Cairo and Butch took cover and returned their fire. Cairo fired and hit him with three shots to the chest, then he laid down cover fire while Butch fired and killed the other man. Two more men came out of the building, firing with AK47s, and forced Cairo and Butch to take cover. Nikki took cover and fired a couple of shots at one.

Two men raised and pointed their weapons and opened fire. Cairo fired several shots in the direction of the men, and they fired back. Nikki fired and hit one with three shots before she moved to cover.

Four men came out of the building and began firing. That was when Nikki saw Wilkes come out of the building. Wilkes fired a few shots at Nikki before he reached cover behind a car. Wilkes raised his weapon and fired until his gun was empty. He ejected the clip and slammed in another. Before he could resume firing, Nikki moved out from cover and took up a position closer to him. He began firing at Nikki.

While the other two men continued firing and blanketed the courtyard with a barrage of bullets, Cairo hit the ground and crawled to where Nikki was shooting it out with Wilkes.

"We need to get outta here!" Cairo shouted.

"No!" Nikki shouted back as she opened fire until she had emptied her clip. She reloaded her weapon. "Cover me," Nikki yelled as Cairo reloaded.

As Cairo fired at Wilkes, Nikki stayed on the ground and positioned herself on the other side of Wilkes. Cairo got to one knee and fired. When another man turned to fire at Cairo, Nikki killed him. Right then, Wilkes came running out from cover.

"He's getting away!" Nikki yelled, and she followed Wilkes, firing.

Cairo and Butch fired at the remaining shooters as they ran for better cover. Butch stood up and fired at the men. Cairo rose up from his cover position and fired. He hit the one man with two shots to the chest. While Butch kept firing, Cairo got up and began firing. He fired and hit another of Wilkes's men with two in the chest. While Cairo covered, Butch reloaded his weapon, and then he shot a man.

Once the shooting ended, Butch looked around for Nikki. "I don't see her."

"She went after Wilkes," Cairo said.

"Come on. We gotta find her," Butch said, and they ran back to their car.

They drove slowly down the streets and saw Nikki running behind Wilkes. They were exchanging gunfire as they ran.

Cairo pointed. "There she is!" he shouted, and Butch sped up.

Wilkes turned and fired at Nikki. She stopped and fired twice, but she missed, and he kept running.

When they got to the corner, Cairo and Butch could hear gunfire. They stopped the car and got out. Nikki was sitting on the ground behind a car as Wilkes fired away from across the street. Cairo and Butch joined Nikki behind the vehicle. When they got to the hood of the car and opened fire, Nikki circled around and killed Wilkes.

Chapter Twenty-nine

It was past midnight when Jorell arrived at Garraway's house. When he parked, he didn't see any lights on inside. He was expected, so he got out of the car and took the bag of money from the back seat. He approached the house. Jorell rang the bell and stood back. Eventually, the porch light came on, and the door opened.

"Come in."

"Thanks."

Garraway closed the door behind him and then led Jorell into the living room. He sat down, and Jorell sat across from him.

"Since you're here,"—Garraway glanced at his watch—"tell me something I actually wanna hear."

Jorell held up the bag with the money.

"What's that?"

"It's the money the kid robbed from the Palace."

"That's a start."

Jorell tossed the bag toward Garraway's feet.

"What else you got?"

"I talked to the kid. He had enough sense to eliminate his shooters."

Garraway shook his head. "What my police source says is that one of them survived the shooting at the club. He's at Presbyterian Hospital under police protection."

"Shit."

"Yeah. Shit. For the time being, he's not talking. Not even to his court-appointed lawyer. But you and I know that can and will change, and he'll start singing like a choir boy."

"Shit," Jorell repeated. "Hitting a man at the hospital while he's under police protection ain't gonna be easy."

"No, it's not. But it is exactly what you're gonna do."

Jorell nodded. "I'll find a way to get it done."

"Of this, I had no doubt." Garraway paused. "What about Wilkes?"

"I told him to lay low. If Nikki hasn't killed him by the end of the week, I'll take care of him myself."

"See that you do," Garraway said and stood up. "Now, if there's nothing else, I'm going back to bed."

"No, Dee, that's all I got."

"Good."

Jorell stood up, and Garraway walked him to the door to leave.

"Good night, Dee."

"Night." Garraway opened the door. "Get this done before it blows up in our faces."

"I'm on it."

Garraway closed the door.

"All I gotta do now is figure out how I'm gonna get it done," Jorell said aloud as he walked back to his car.

The nurse was wearing scrubs that were way too tight for her. Her ass and tits were big, her hips were wide, and she was swinging it hard as she passed by the officer stationed outside Wilkes's shooter's room. She was pushing a cart that was filled with medical supplies. As she passed the officer, she stared at him flirtatiously and winked. She purposely wasn't watching where she was going and took a wrong step. It caused her to fall to the floor, pulling the supply cart down with her. The officer rushed to help her.

"Are you all right?" He extended his hand to her.

"I think so."

As the two of them placed the supplies back on the cart, another nurse went into the room with Wilkes's man.

"What are you doing?" Wilkes's man asked as she glanced at his chart.

"I'm giving you something for pain," she said, pulling a syringe from her pocket.

"About time. I've been pressing this damn button, trying to get something for pain for hours," he said as she approached the bed.

She inserted the empty syringe into the medical injection port and looked into the man's eyes as she shot an air bubble into his vein, creating a venous air embolism. When the air bubble entered the vein, it traveled to his brain, heart, and lungs, causing him to have a heart attack, and he went into respiratory failure. With her task completed, she left the room, signaling to the other nurse impersonator that it was time to get out of there.

"Thank you for your help," the first nurse said and rushed off down the hall as the police officer returned to his post. That was when the alarms started going off.

After Nikki killed Cedric, Ice Man had slid into his position. He was at the trap house the night Nikki hit them, but he was slow getting his gun, or maybe he was just in no hurry to join the firefight. Either way, the Ice Man got outside in time to see Cairo and Butch drive away. When he was informed that Wilkes was dead, Ice Man slid into the top spot.

However, with his newfound power came demands for him to do something about Wilkes's killing. As far as he was concerned, Wilkes was a fool who got sloppy and needed to be replaced. He thought that going to war with Nikki Marx was a mistake because Cedric was a fool, too, and he needed to die. In the few days since Nikki killed Wilkes, things had been quiet, so he saw no reason to upset things by retaliating against Nikki. But he was getting a lot of pressure from what were now his men, and Ice Man gave in to the pressure to respond.

"What you wanna do?" he asked Boggs, the man who had been applying the pressure.

"Me and Luka, we get a couple of guys. We follow her and get her in an ambush."

Ice looked long and hard at Boggs. "You sure you can handle it?"

"Yeah, man, I'm sure. All I need is a chance to prove it."

Ice pointed in his face. "Don't fuck this up."

"I won't."

"All right. It's your show." Ice pointed in his face again. "Don't fuck this up. Wilkes fucked up, and you see how well that went for him."

As the days passed, despite her suspicions about Arya, Nikki seemed more willing to accept that she had avenged her brother's murder. Now, it was time to try to move forward. She decided that she would make an offer on the restaurant that she, Naomi, and J.R. had looked at before he died. An appointment was made with the real estate agent, and Nikki was on her way to meet her.

As she drove, Nikki thought about killing Wilkes. It caused her to think back to her first kill. She was nineteen and anxious to step up and prove herself to Barlowe. He gave her what was supposed to be an easy pickup. Despite what Barlowe said about how easy it would be, Nikki was nervous. J.R. was too young, and there was no Cairo and Butch those days. When she arrived at the pickup, she noticed that things weren't the way Barlowe said they would be. That was her first red flag, so Nikki proceeded carefully.

"You got the money?" Nikki asked with her hand on her gun.

"Nope," the man said and raised his weapon.

They shot it out for a while before Nikki killed him. Then, once she calmed down and caught her breath, she searched the place, found the money, and got out of there. Her heart was still pounding in her chest as she made her escape. Barlowe was proud of his young protege.

"You did what you had to do."

After that, Nikki was involved in a couple of shootouts, not actually knowing if she killed anybody or not. Enter Stan "the Man" Hillman, a low-rent drug dealer who, like Nikki, was looking for a chance to show and prove. The big break came when he and his partner were assigned to sell two kilos to a woman named Pravleen MacQuoid.

At the meeting, Stan the Man shot and killed MacQuoid and his partner. He took the money and the drugs and went into hiding. However, Stan The Man made two mistakes. Once he checked into a motel and stayed there, he didn't change rooms or locations. His second mistake was that Stan the Man had a thing for working girls. He had been ghost for weeks before he made the mistake of calling Amanda Reese and asking her to send over a couple of women. He used a fake name, but one of the women knew Stan the Man. She reported his whereabouts to Amanda Reese, who quickly informed Barlowe. He sent Nikki with orders to kill him.

When Nikki arrived at the motel, Amanda Reese was waiting there for her. She told Nikki what room he was in.

"How long has she been in there with him?"

Amanda Reese looked at her watch. "She should be coming out soon."

"Thanks. You can go now. I'll take it from here," Nikki said, and she walked toward the building. She leaned on the railing with her gun in her hand and waited.

Once the door opened a few minutes later, and the working girl came out, Nikki stepped up quickly.

"Nikki," Stan the Man said with the quiet resolve that he was about to die.

Nikki motioned for him to step back, and once she closed the door, the gun was in his face. "Where's the money and the product?"

"Fuck you, Nikki. I ain't telling you shit!" he shouted defiantly.

Nikki took a deep breath and shot him twice in the chest.

This was different than shooting a man in the heat of battle. This time, Nikki had to stand before her target, look him in the eyes, and pull the trigger. As Stan the Man fell to the floor, Nikki looked down at the body of the man she'd just killed. She stood there for a while before she lowered her weapon and cleared the room.

As the light turned yellow, the car that was in front of Nikki, which was driven by Ice, slammed on its brakes. As Nikki hit her brakes to avoid the crash, a cargo van pulled up alongside her. Nikki saw the guns and ducked. The side door of the cargo van slid open quickly, but it gave Nikki time to get her gun and make her way to the passenger seat. When Boggs and Luka got out and began firing at her with automatic weapons. Nikki opened the passenger door, got out of the car, and crawled away to safety before she started to run. They were so preoccupied with firing at the car they didn't see her.

When the shooting stopped, Ice, Boggs, and Luka approached the car.

"She's gone," Boggs said when they looked in the car.

"Find her! She couldn't have gotten far," Ice said.

Boggs and Luka began running down the street. "There she is!" Boggs shouted and fired at her.

Nikki kept running until she reached the corner. She stopped, turned quickly, and fired off a couple of shots. It forced Boggs and Luka to take cover. When they were about to return fire, Nikki took off running again. She rounded the corner and ducked into a bar to hide.

From where she was standing, Nikki could see the window and saw Boggs and Luka stop in front of the bar. She watched as they talked, and then they came into the bar. Nikki was looking around the bar for a place to hide or a way out of there when Boggs and Luka went to the bar.

"You see a woman run in here?" Luka asked the bartender.

"No." He dropped a bar napkin in front of them. "What are you drinking?"

"Two shots of Hennessy," Boggs said.

"We don't have time for that," Luka said.

"Ain't gonna take but a minute. Ice will be all right."

When Nikki noticed that they weren't looking for her, she knew that was her chance. She was going to slide past them and out the door, but then she had a better idea. With her gun at her side, Nikki walked up behind Boggs and Luka. She put the barrel of her gun to the back of Boggs's head and pulled the trigger.

"Oh, shit!" Luka turned to Nikki and shouted before she shot him in the face.

Chapter Thirty

Nikki left the bar and walked quickly down the street to the nearest subway station. When the train came, she got on. When Nikki got off the train, she walked to Cairo and Butch's apartment and rang the bell.

"Just a minute!" she heard Cairo yell, and shortly thereafter, he opened the door to let Nikki into the apartment.

"What's up, Nik-Nik?" he asked as Nikki came in.

"Somebody just tried to kill me. That's what's up." Nikki plopped down on the couch.

"What?" Cairo asked as he sat down on the couch next to her.

"Somebody tried to kill me."

"What?" Butch asked when he came out of his room.

"Somebody just tried to kill Nikki," Cairo said.

Just then, Cairo's bedroom door opened, and Rah-Rah came into the living room naked.

"Oh. I'm sorry." She had just woken up, so her eyes were red, and her hair was matted to her head. "I didn't know you were here, Nikki," she said and turned to go back into the room. She stopped at the door. "You got a little something I can smoke?"

"Yeah, yeah. In a minute," Cairo said and waved her back into the room.

"Okay," she said and then stood there for a second or two before going back into the room.

"What happened?" Butch asked, and Nikki told them about the ambush. "Why didn't you call us?"

"I know. I know. I should have called. It won't happen again, I promise."

"Good. From now on, where you go, I go," Cairo said.

"Agreed."

"You know who it was?" Butch asked.

"I don't know their names, but they were some more of Wilkes's people."

"What you gonna do now?" Cairo asked.

"Right now? Right now, I'm gonna go talk to Barlowe. Tell him what happened."

"Give me a minute to get dressed," Butch said, and he went back into his room.

Cairo stood up and went to get something for Rah-Rah to smoke and took it into the room.

"What's up with that?" Nikki asked when he came out.

"House pussy."

"I see." Nikki nodded. "Ain't she Shekira's friend?"

"Yup," Cairo said as Butch came out of the room.

"Ready?"

Nikki stood up. "Let's go."

When they arrived at Barlowe's house, Cairo and Butch waited in the living room with Arya while Nikki went into the library.

"How's it going, Nikki?"

"Somebody tried to kill me."

"Again?" Barlowe shook his head in disgust. "Who was it this time, more of Wilkes's people?"

"Yeah," Nikki said and told Barlowe the story of how she barely escaped when the shooting started.

"This has gone on long enough." Barlowe took out his phone. "Time to put a stop to this."

"Who are you calling?"

"Marques. It's Pete. Is Duncan back yet?"

"Yeah, Pete, he's back," Jorell said and looked at Garraway. Garraway shook his head. He didn't want to talk to Barlowe. "But he's not available right now. What can I do for you?"

"Me and him need to talk." Barlowe chuckled. "I know it's been a while, but we need to talk face-to-face."

"I'll give him the message and get back to you."

"Thanks, Marques," Barlowe said, and Jorell ended the call.

"He'll get back to me about a sit-down. I'll let you know when I hear back from them."

"You bringing me along to this sit-down?"

"Yes. It's about you, so yeah, you're coming with me."

"Okay." Nikki stood up. "I won't do anything until I hear from you," Nikki said, and once she got Cairo and Butch away from Arya, they left the house.

Later that evening, Nikki was in the office at the Palace when Butch tapped on the door and came in.

"What's up?" Nikki asked when she saw the strange look on his face.

"Duncan Garraway is here to see you."

"How many people he got with him?" Nikki asked, getting her gun from the desk drawer.

"Believe it or not, he came alone."

"You're bullshittin'?"

"No, I am not." Cairo chuckled. "He's not even armed."

"Bold," Nikki said. "But I respect that." She put the gun down on the desk and stood up. "Show Mr. Garraway in."

"You got it," Butch said, and he left the office.

A few seconds later, the door opened, and he showed Duncan Garraway into the office.

"Please, come in, Mr. Garraway."

"Thank you," Garraway said and stopped to look at Nikki.

It had been fifteen years since he'd last seen her. In those years, she had grown into a beautiful woman. That night, she was wearing a Cinq à Sept Ida beaded-trim satin crop, single-button jacket, matching Doris beaded-hem satin miniskirt, and Prada logo satin platform ankle-strap sandals.

"Please forgive me for staring. The last time I saw you, you were a little girl in pigtails and bangs."

"That was a long time ago." Nikki extended her hand graciously. "Please have a seat and tell me what I can do for you."

Garraway sat down. "I got a call from Pete earlier today, and since I knew he wanted to talk about you, I thought I'd cut out the middleman and come directly to you."

"Fair enough." Her respect for him grew. "Where do we start?"

"Let's start with you telling me why circumstances have brought us to the point where Pete Barlowe felt it necessary to call me after all these years. Not once, but twice."

"Somebody murdered my brother J.R.," Nikki began.

"I am very sorry for your loss."

"Thank you. I had reason to believe that Wilkes was involved."

"Mind if I ask why?"

"Cards on the table?"

"Go ahead, but before you do, I can assure you that Wilkes didn't have anything to do with your brother's murder."

Nikki paused to take that statement in. "I was told it was in retaliation for J.R.'s crew robbing one of Wilkes's spots and killing his people. He reached out to a guy named Cromwell to set it up."

"Cromwell?"

"You know him?"

"Unfortunately, I do." Garraway nodded. "I haven't heard that one, but I promise you, I will ask some questions. But I know for a fact that Cromwell is Chicago."

Nikki pointed at Garraway. "See. I heard that, too. It's what's been bothering me since I first heard it."

"I'm willing to say what's done is done. Wilkes is dead. You and I don't have a problem. You have my word that we had nothing to do with your brother's murder. So, I'm asking if you and I can move forward from here, and we all go back to making money."

"We can do that. But I'm not interested in going back to the way things were."

"Okay. What did you have in mind?"

"Barlowe told me that when my father was alive, the three of you formed a group to settle disputes, distribution problems, and other issues."

"The Council."

"Yes, the Council." Nikki nodded. "That's what I'm interested in. I think issues like the one we just had may have been avoided."

"I think you're wise beyond your years, Nikki Marx."

"Thank you."

"Yes. I am interested in that, too." Garraway pointed at Nikki. "In fact, it was what I was hoping would come of this when I made the decision to come here."

"Do you mind me asking why you dissolved the Council?"

"I didn't. Pete blew that up after your father died."

"He did?"

"Yes, he did."

"I always thought it was you," Nikki said and wondered what else she had been wrong about. "Why did he blow it up after my father died?"

"I don't know if this is my story to tell you, Nikki."

"Apparently, nobody else has told me the story, so you might as well." Nikki paused. "We agreed, cards on the table."

"We did, didn't we?" Garraway stared at Nikki for what seemed like a long time. "How do I say this?"

"In English."

Garraway laughed. "You have your father's quick wit. You look like him, too." He took a deep breath. "One night, I was at the Palace when Pete came in. He was looking rough. I asked him what was wrong, and he said it was nothing. About an hour later, your father shows up there, and he goes after Pete."

"Went after him how?"

"Eddie beat the shit outta Pete that night. He kept saying, 'I'm sorry. I didn't mean it,' but your pops kept hitting him. Then he said, 'If you come near my wife again, I'll kill you.'" Garraway paused. "Eddie left after that, and I heard Pete say, 'Not if I kill you first.'"

"What are you saying?"

"That the next night, Eddie was shot to death in front of your house."

"Are you telling me that Uncle Pete had my father killed?"

"No, Nikki, I'm not saying that at all. You heard what I said. One night, Pete threatened to kill him first, and the next night, Eddie was dead."

"Did you ask him if he had my father killed?"

"Of course I did. Pete told me he didn't, and I didn't have much choice but to accept it and move forward. But the day after the funeral, Pete dissolved the Council, and we haven't spoken since."

There was silence in the office. The only sound was the house band, Future Shock, playing "Payback," the James Brown classic. Nikki looked at Garraway.

"I need a drink." Nikki got up and went to the bar in the office. "Can I get you one?"

"Whatever you're drinking is fine."

Nikki picked up a bottle of Stolichnaya Gold. "Is vodka all right?"

"Vodka is fine."

Nikki poured the two glasses and returned to the desk. Once she handed Garraway his drink, she sat down in the chair next to him.

"How do I know what you're telling me is the truth?" Nikki sipped her drink. "You're right. I haven't seen you since I was ten years old, and you come in here and tell me this story about Barlowe and my father."

Nikki thought for a second. *It would explain Mommy's hatred of Barlowe.*

"Why should I believe you?"

"You are absolutely right. You have no reason to believe me." Garraway shot his vodka. "However, there are two people who know the truth."

Nikki nodded. "True. But to this point, neither Barlowe nor Mommy have seen fit to tell me the truth."

"Maybe it's time you asked them about it."

"Believe me, I will."

Chapter Thirty-one

Fifteen Years Ago

Naomi went into the bathroom and turned on the shower. Once it reached the perfect temperature, she stepped in and let the water caress her body. As Naomi slid the loofah over her skin, she thought about what she was going to wear that evening. Eddie was taking her to dinner.

Naomi thought about the night before and the love-making she'd experienced, and her hand settled between her thighs. It wasn't long before she was petting her mound and coaxing her lips to open. Naomi put the loofah down and allowed her hands to caress the soap across her nipples, down to her stomach, and in between her thighs. She ran her finger up and down her slit, then dipped a finger inside. Once Naomi felt her walls tighten around her fingers, she got out of the shower, dried, and wrapped a towel around herself.

She had selected an Alexander McQueen knotted crepe evening gown and had just laid it out on the bed when she heard the doorbell ring. She grabbed her Kiki de Montparnasse silk kimono robe and went to look at the security monitor. When she saw that it was Pete

Barlowe, her husband Eddie's partner, she went to the door to let him in.

"Naomi," Barlowe said with his eyes wide open when he saw her.

The silk robe clung to her damp body, and therefore, it left little to the imagination. Barlowe pushed his way past her. It didn't take her long to know that he'd been drinking. She'd seen him like this before.

"Where's my boy, Fast Eddie?" he slurred.

"He's not here."

He got in her face. "Where is he?"

Naomi stepped back, but Barlowe kept coming toward her. "He didn't say where he was going or when he'd be back. Can I do something for you?" she asked, but she continued to move away from Barlowe.

"You are so beautiful, Naomi."

"Thank you."

He took a step closer to Naomi. "Give me a kiss."

When he reached for her, Naomi pushed him back. "You're drunk."

"Come on. Just a little kiss ain't gonna hurt nobody," Barlowe said, and he lunged at her.

She moved out of the way, and he stumbled and almost fell on the couch. "Stop it, Pete." Naomi moved around the couch with Barlowe coming at her. "You're drunk, and you need to leave."

This time, when Barlowe lunged at Naomi, she didn't move fast enough, and he grabbed her. She struggled against him, but he was too strong for her, and he easily overpowered Naomi.

"Stop it, Pete!" Naomi shouted as she hit him over and over in his chest.

He forced her onto the couch. "Just a little kiss," Barlowe said, jerking open the sash of her robe and forcing himself between her legs.

Naomi got still and stared into his eyes. "Please, Pete. Don't do this. I'm begging you," she said quietly.

Barlowe's eyes closed, and he bounced up. "I'm sorry." He backed up and almost stumbled to the floor. "I'm sorry," he said before he turned and ran out of the house.

Naomi stood up slowly and re-tied her sash, glad that things hadn't gone any further, and she started to cry. Tears were still staining her cheeks when Eddie came home.

"What's wrong?" he asked, rushing to his wife's side.

"Nothing," Naomi said quickly and tried to wipe away her tears.

He sat down on the couch next to her. "What's wrong?" Eddie asked again, and this time, Naomi told her husband the truth.

"What happened?"

"He was drunk, Eddie."

"He? Who's he?"

"Pete."

"What happened?"

Naomi said nothing.

"Please, tell me what happened. What did Pete do?" he asked, not expecting to hear the worst.

"Pete tried to rape me, Eddie."

He bounced up angrily from the couch.

"He was drunk, Eddie!"

"Muthafucka! I'll kill him!" Eddie shouted and rushed out of the house.

Eddie went to Barlowe's house, and not finding him there, he went to their construction office, to Marquee, and the XL before he saw him at the bar at the Palace. He was sitting there with Duncan Garraway, and Eddie could tell that he had indeed been drinking.

"Muthafucka!" he shouted and rushed toward Barlowe.

"I'm sorry, Eddie," Barlowe said, and they struggled for a while.

Eddie hit Barlowe with blow after blow until he went down. Eddie stood over Barlowe and kicked him a few times before he pulled Barlowe up.

"I'm sorry, Eddie. I didn't know what I was doing."

Eddie looked around for something to beat Barlowe with. He picked up a chair and hit him with it. Barlowe tried to cover his head as Eddie hit him over and over again. Eddie dropped the chair and got on top of Barlowe. He hit him several times in the face before he grabbed Barlowe by his shirt and began pounding his head into the floor.

At that point, Garraway had seen enough. He pulled Eddie off of Barlowe, who struggled to get to his feet. Barlowe's face was a bloody mess.

"Let me go!" Eddie said calmly and stopped struggling. Garraway let him go.

Eddie pointed at Barlowe. "If you come near my wife again, I'll kill you!" he shouted and left the Palace.

Garraway looked at Barlowe trying to catch his breath as Eddie walked away. "Not if I kill you first," Barlowe said and sat down at the bar.

The following evening, when Eddie got home and parked in the driveway, a car pulled up quickly in front of the house. Before Eddie could react, he saw the gun come out of the window. The shooter fired six shots. Each bullet hit Eddie in the chest and head. When Naomi came running out of the house, she found Eddie lying in a pool of his own blood. She called the police and an ambulance, but when the first responders arrived, they pronounced Eddie Marx dead.

Chapter Thirty-two

Nikki didn't leave the Palace until the club closed. Cairo and Butch drove her to her mother's house. On the way, Nikki remained quiet. When they asked her what Garraway wanted, she replied with a single word.

"Peace."

They had known Nikki long enough to know that there was no point trying to get her to talk. She would tell them what was going on when she was ready. However, both knew that whatever was on her mind was something serious.

When she got to her mother's house, Nikki told Cairo and Butch that she would call them in the morning when she was ready to leave.

"Anything we can do for you before we go?" Cairo asked.

"No," Nikki said, walking to the house with her head hanging low.

Naomi woke up in the morning and got out of bed. As had become her custom, she went to see if Nikki was in the house. She peeked into the room, and when she saw that her daughter was there, Naomi padded her way to the kitchen. She started a pot of coffee and put on the bacon. It had been a while, and knowing how much she enjoyed them, Naomi decided to make waffles for breakfast that morning.

As she got the waffle iron ready, Naomi took a minute to think about how much she was enjoying having Nikki in the house. She was excited about getting a chance to work with Nikki on opening the new restaurant. She only wished that J.R. was still with them so they could do it as a family.

When the food was finished cooking, Naomi was surprised that Nikki hadn't made her way to the kitchen. She would smell the bacon cooking, and that was usually enough to wake her up. Naomi was going to wake her up, but then she changed her mind.

Maybe she's tired, Naomi thought, and decided to let her sleep.

She covered the food, poured herself a second cup of coffee, and sat down to wait and have breakfast with Nikki when she woke up. It was over an hour later when Nikki came dragging into the kitchen.

"Good morning, Nikki."

"Morning, Mommy," Nikki said, getting a cup from the cabinet and pouring herself a cup of coffee.

Naomi stood up and put their food in the microwave. "You want one waffle or two?"

"One." Nikki sat down at the table.

She looked at her mother and wondered how she would ask what she wanted to know. What she now had to know. She knew that it was something that Naomi didn't want to talk about, but she had to know.

"Sit down, Mommy. There's something I need to talk to you about."

Naomi set the plate in front of Nikki and fixed her own. "This sounds serious."

"It is."

"Oh, okay," Naomi said and sat down with her plate.

Nikki grabbed the bottle of strawberry syrup and poured it over her waffles. "I talked to Duncan Garraway last night."

"Duncan?" Naomi questioned, and Nikki could tell by the look in her eyes that the mere mention of his name made her uncomfortable. "Where did you see him?"

"He came to the Palace to talk to me."

"What did he want?"

"Barlowe called him about the two of them sitting down to, you know, to put a stop to this rampage I've been on."

"You have been on a rampage. Your brother is dead, so I understood, but it has gone far enough."

"I know. And I'm done with it now. Yeah, I still got some questions, and some things still don't seem right to me, but I gave my word, so it's over. At least until I find out what really happened to J.R."

"I understand."

"We agreed to restart the Council so we can talk before we start shooting at each other."

"I think that a good idea. What did Pete think about that? You know he hasn't spoken to Duncan in years."

"I haven't told him yet."

"Since he handed you power, he couldn't have anything to say about it, but knowing that nigga, he will."

"No doubt. If he doesn't, I know Arya will have a lot to say about it."

"Fuck her and the horse her bitch ass rode in on," Naomi said.

"For sure." Nikki got up to pour a second cup of coffee. "Yeah, Garraway thought that restarting the Council was a great idea."

"It was part of your father's legacy."

"He agreed that issues like the one we just had could have been avoided." Nikki sat down with her coffee. "So, I asked him why he dissolved the Council, and he said that he didn't. He said Barlowe dissolved the Council after Daddy was murdered."

Naomi looked at Nikki. "He told you, didn't he?"

Nikki nodded. "But I need to know from you what really happened that day."

Naomi exhaled and stood up.

"Where are you going?"

"To get some coffee," she said, holding up her cup as she walked to the pot. She came back to the table and sat down.

"What happened that day to make Daddy go beat Barlowe?"

"Pete came by here that day while your father was gone. He was drunk."

Nikki's facial expression changed. "What happened?" she asked and braced herself for what she was about to hear.

"He was drunk, and he tried to rape me. When your father came home, I told him what happened, and he went after Pete."

"Did you know that he threatened to kill Barlowe if he came near you again?"

Naomi nodded, and tears filled her eyes. "Duncan told me."

"So you know that he threatened to kill Daddy?"

"He told me that too."

"And the next day, Daddy is murdered in front of this house, and you didn't think that Barlowe had something to do with it?"

"I was sure that he did!" Naomi shouted. "I was sure, Duncan was sure, everybody was sure that bastard had something to do with it. One day, he threatens to kill him, and the next day, he's dead. But we couldn't prove it."

"Why didn't you tell us the truth?"

"Because I was afraid. He had your father killed. I thought that telling you kids or even mentioning what I thought would get us all killed. And I had to protect you kids."

Nikki nodded. "This explains a lot."

"I'm sorry, Nikki. I did what I thought was right." She paused. "After it happened, Caroline was right there for me. She was my best friend, and she did so much for you kids because I was having a tough time coping with your father's murder. And then Pete really stepped up, and I couldn't tell whether it was because he felt guilty about what he had done and this was his way of making up for it, or if was he doing it because he was a good man who was honoring his friend's memory, or it was something that Caroline made him. I didn't know, and after a while, it didn't matter. You kids were taken care of, and that's all that mattered to me."

"It matters to me!"

"I know it does." Naomi witnessed the angry look on her daughter's face. "What are you going to do now that you know the truth?"

"Nothing for the time being. But he's been lying to me all my life. It's time I found out what else he's been lying to me about. So, no, I'm not going to run over there and put two in his head if that's what you were thinking."

"I was. That's exactly what I thought you were going to do."

"No. But at some point, Barlowe is gonna have to answer to me for Daddy's murder. Until then, it's business as usual, like I don't know anything about any of this."

Chapter Thirty-three

When Nikki finished eating, she picked up her plate and took it to the sink. Then, she took out her phone and made a call.

"Morning," Cairo answered.

"How are you doing this morning, Cairo?"

"I'm good. What's up?"

"Come get me."

"I'm outside."

"What you doing outside?"

"Waiting for you to call."

"Butchie with you?"

"Nope. He was still asleep when I left."

"Come inside."

"Cool," Cairo said and ended the conversation.

Nikki went to the door to let Cairo into the house and took him to the kitchen.

"Good morning, Cairo."

"Good morning, Mrs. Marx."

"Have some breakfast?" Naomi asked.

"Thank you," Cairo said and sat down at the table.

"I'm going to shower and get dressed," Nikki said to Cairo and left the kitchen.

"You want some eggs and grits to go with those waffles?"

"I wouldn't want you to go to any trouble for me, Mrs. Marx."

"No trouble at all," Nikki heard Naomi say on her way to the shower.

Once Nikki was dressed and Cairo finished eating, they drove to the apartment to pick up Butch, and then they drove to Barlowe's house. Nikki didn't know exactly what she was going to say to him, but there were questions that she needed answers to, and Barlowe was the only one who could provide them. She had decided that she wasn't going to tell him what Garraway told her about his involvement in her father's murder.

Nikki looked at Cairo and Butch. They needed to know what was going on, but she wasn't going to tell them about Barlowe's involvement.

"Garraway told me that he didn't think Wilkes had anything to do with J.R. getting killed."

"You believe him?" Butch asked.

"I don't know. I mean, he doesn't have any reason to lie to me about it at this point." Nikki chuckled. "The nigga's dead. And he was sure that Cromwell was in Chicago."

"So, does he have any idea who set J.R. up?" Cairo asked.

"No."

"So what are we gonna do?" Butch asked.

"Not we. You."

"Me?"

"Yeah. I want you to go to Chicago and find Cromwell."

"On it," Butch said. "I need to pack."

"Cool those jets," Nikki said. "Let me talk to Barlowe first, then we'll get you going."

"Cool."

When they arrived at Barlowe's house, he and Arya were celebrating an anniversary and had French food catered for lunch. They were dining on moules frites and trout amandine when he was informed that Nikki was there to see him.

"Afternoon," Barlowe said when they were shown into the dining room.

"I need to talk to you," Nikki said.

"I'm listening."

"I need to talk to you alone," Nikki said.

Barlowe glanced at Arya, picked up his napkin, and wiped his mouth before he stood up.

"I'll be right back," he said and kissed Arya on the forehead. "Let's walk."

"I'm right behind you," Nikki said and followed Barlowe as he walked out the double doors to the pool deck.

"Sorry to interrupt your celebration."

Barlowe chuckled. "No, you're not. If you were sorry, you wouldn't have done it."

"Fine. I didn't intentionally ruin your celebration. What are you celebrating anyway?"

"We met sixteen years ago."

"Congratulations."

"Thanks. Now, what did you want to talk about?"

"I had a visitor at the Palace last night."

"Really, who was that?"

"Duncan Garraway."

"What?"

Nikki paid close attention to the way Barlowe's expression changed at the mention of his name.

"Duncan came to the club?" He paused. "To talk to you?"

"Yes. Garraway said that he got your message, and since I was the issue, he came to talk to me about it."

"Why didn't you call me?"

"I didn't think I needed to call you. Why would I need to?" Nikki asked with attitude.

"What did he say, Nikki?"

It was apparent to Nikki that Barlowe was, at best, apprehensive, and at worst, he was scared about what Garraway had told her.

"He said that to his knowledge, Wilkes didn't have anything to do with J.R.'s murder."

"You believe him?"

"I don't know. That's what I wanted to talk to you about."

"What's that?"

"I don't know that man. But you do."

"I do."

"Can I trust him?"

Barlowe walked alongside Nikki, not speaking for a second or two before he said, "Duncan Garraway is a lot of things, but he is a man of his word. If he told you something, it's a fact, or he believes it to be a fact. Duncan Garraway is a man of honor. Ain't too many men like him."

"That's good to know."

"So, how'd you leave it with him?"

"We talked about restarting the Council. We agreed that if we had been talking, all of the issues we've had could have been avoided."

"I think that's a good idea."

"I do, too." Nikki paused. "I was kinda surprised when he suggested it. You know, seeing that he was the one that disbanded the Council after Daddy died."

"I guess he saw the value in it again after all these years."

"I guess so."

Nikki was disappointed. She had given him an opportunity to tell her the truth that he was the one who disbanded the Council, but he chose to continue lying to her. It told her all that she needed to know.

"I'm gonna let you get back to your celebration."

"You be careful with Duncan."

"You just said he was an honorable man."

"I did, but that doesn't mean that you shouldn't be careful dealing with him."

"Understood. Thank you, Uncle Pete."

"Anything for you, Nikki. You know that," Barlowe said, feeling that his secret was safe, at least for the time being. If Garraway had told her that he thought Barlowe was involved in her father's murder, there would have been no conversation. Nikki would have come in with her guns blazing.

"Yeah, I know."

"Where you off to now?" Barlowe asked as he and Nikki went back into the house.

"Airport. Butch is taking a little working vacation."

"Really? Where's he going?"

Nikki and Barlowe walked back into the house where Cairo and Butch were waiting with Arya.

"Chicago. Now that I know that Wilkes wasn't involved, I need to find Cromwell," Nikki said and glanced in Arya's direction.

"Good idea."

"I'll let you know what he finds out." She turned to Cairo and Butch and said, "Come on. Let's go."

Once Nikki left with Cairo and Butch, Barlowe and Arya could get back to their anniversary celebration, but neither seemed to be in a celebratory mood any longer. Whether or not Garraway had told Nikki, he knew the truth of what happened that day. It had haunted him every day since, and he'd tried his best to make up for it on each of those days. However, no matter what he did or how hard he tried, Barlowe knew that he could never truly make amends for his actions.

What he remembered most about that day was being drunk. Barlowe couldn't say for sure why he went to Eddie's house that afternoon. His memories of the attempted rape were a blur. He remembered being on top of Naomi, her staring into his eyes and struggling against him.

He could still hear her words: *"Please, Pete. Don't do this."*

Barlowe remembered running out of there, but not how he got to the Palace. That was when he realized what he had done, and the regret began to creep up on him.

Naomi was beautiful in those days. *Still is*, Barlowe thought, but since Arya was sitting next to him, he chose not to say aloud. From the time he and Eddie were introduced to Naomi, Barlowe had wanted her. For a short time in those early days, he thought he had a chance. But Naomi only had eyes for Eddie, and he for her.

"I knew she was the one the second I kissed her," was what Eddie told Barlowe.

That didn't stop Barlowe from wanting her. Even when he met and eventually married Caroline, who was equally as beautiful as Naomi, she always seemed like a consolation prize. Naomi and Eddie were so in love with each other, sharing the kind of love that Barlowe could only envy.

Barlowe thought about that hot, muggy day. Naomi had just gotten out of the shower. When she put on her robe to answer the door, the material clung to her body. A smile crept across his lips. She looked so good that day, and the thought made him feel disgusted with himself almost immediately. He had come close to raping his best friend's wife, and that was nothing to smile about.

Barlowe knew it was wrong, and he knew that once Eddie found out what he had done, there would be consequences, and they would be extreme. He had sobered up enough to realize what he had done by the time Eddie arrived. He could have defended himself and put up some resistance to the beating that he took at Eddie's hands, but at that moment, he felt what he had done was indefensible, and he deserved the beating he took.

"If you come near my wife again, I'll kill you!"

"Not if I kill you first."

Those words, "not if I kill you first," rang in his ears like an echo for years. Those words and the actions that they led him to changed so many lives. There were times when Barlowe wondered: if Duncan Garraway and all those people in the club hadn't been there to witness the beating, would his response have been the same? He was embarrassed and humiliated in public. His pride demanded a response.

When Garraway left the Palace, Barlowe had made the call to a friend in New Jersey.

"I need someone taken care of."

"Who'd you have in mind?"

"Eddie Marx," Barlowe said, and the man laughed. "What's funny?"

"I just knew it would come to this one day. When and where?"

"Tomorrow night. In front of his house."

"Done."

And that was it. The following night, Eddie Marx was murdered in front of his house. Barlowe didn't think anymore about it until he got the screaming and crying call from Naomi. He acted as if he were shocked and swore to kill whoever was responsible. It was as if he hadn't ordered the hit himself.

Barlowe remembered feeling shaken and remorseful by the loss of a friend. He thought about his vow to find who was responsible and kill them, and his promise to always take care of Naomi and the kids. Maybe there was a part of him that thought he could fill that void in Naomi's life. He would be there to comfort her in her time of loss. That fantasy ended the day after Eddie's funeral.

"You had him killed, didn't you? You bastard!"

He could still hear Naomi screaming with tears rolling down her cheeks while she pounded her fists into his chest.

"I hate you!"

All he could do was hold her and reiterate his promise to always take care of her and the children. He had done his best for them. Barlowe saw Nikki and J.R. as his children. All he could do was help Nikki find out who had really killed her brother.

Chapter Thirty-four

As for Arya, she had lost her appetite and no longer felt like celebrating either. She was feeling pretty proud of herself for the way she had manipulated the circumstances. Arya had orchestrated J.R.'s murder and had cast suspicion on Wilkes. Everything was going as planned, until Nikki talked to Garraway. Maybe she should have used one of her more-than-willing minions to make the call to set up J.R. and had them killed once they completed their task.

"Why do you look like the cat that swallowed the chicken?" Barlowe asked Arya.

"Huh?"

"What's wrong with you?"

"Nothing. Just a little indigestion is all," Arya lied to Barlowe. "I'll be fine." She got up. "I'm going to lie down for a while."

Arya went to their room and shut the door. She sat down on the bed and took out her phone to make a call.

"What's up, sexy?" Remy answered

"We need to talk."

"Where and when?"

"The lobby lounge at the Ludlow Hotel."

"When?"

"Tonight, at nine."

"See you tonight, sexy," Remy said, and he ended the call.

At nine forty-five, dressed in a Valentino Garavani drap coat and 3x1 Kaya split-cuff coated skinny jeans, Arya arrived at the Lobby Lounge, an airy, softly lit bar with cozy couches. They didn't stay in the lounge for long.

"We have a problem," Arya said as soon as they entered a hotel room.

"What's that?"

"Garraway told Nikki that Wilkes didn't have anything to do with J.R.'s murder."

"Garraway?" Remy questioned. "I thought him and Barlowe were mortal enemies."

"They were. But with Nikki going hard at them, Barlowe felt the need to reach out to him to make peace."

"And you couldn't stop him?"

"No, I couldn't. And now she's questioning the call from Cromwell. She sent Butch to Chicago to look for him."

"Shit. That's not good." Remy shook his head. "Damn it, Arya. I knew putting that shit on Cromwell was a mistake the second you said it."

"Then why didn't you say something about it then?"

Remy didn't answer. He sat stone-faced, looking at Arya. She sucked her teeth.

"What's done is done. Too late to second-guess ourselves. We need to find a way out of this."

"What's your plan?"

"We need to kill Nikki."

Remy chuckled. "When you say *we*, you mean *me*. I need to kill Nikki for you."

"No, lover." Arya smiled. "You need to kill Nikki for us."

Remy nodded. "What's in it for me?"

"You mean other than killing her before she kills you?"

"Yeah, Arya, other than that? What's in it for me?"

"Once Nikki is out of the way, someone needs to step in and run things for the old man. I can't think of anybody better for that than you."

"I should be running things for Barlowe now. Not Nikki. She didn't deserve for him to hand her power like that."

"You're right. She didn't. But since that's what he did, you need to kill her and take what could have been yours." Arya shook her head. "I've never understood why he is so dedicated to them fuckin' kids, but he is, and it clouds his judgment."

Remy chuckled. "I thought only you could cloud his judgment."

"Funny."

"Yeah, I know. That's me. Mr. fuckin' happy."

"Will you do it?"

"Yeah, I'll take care of it for us."

"Thank you."

"I'm telling you now, this little arrangement is fine for now, but you and I need to be taking steps to move Barlowe to retirement, or we retire him."

"That's exactly what I had in mind, lover. But not until we solidify our position. Once we've done that, it will just be you and me."

"On top of the world."

"On top of the world where we've always belonged," Arya said and got out of bed.

"You gotta go right away?" Remy pulled back the sheet and stroked himself. "I was hoping we could go around one more time before you go."

"Sorry, lover. I gotta get back," she said and went into the bathroom to shower and get dressed to go home to Barlowe.

Remy watched the door close and looked down at his hard dick. "What you looking at me for?"

Things were quiet for the rest of the week. Nikki focused her attention on opening the new restaurant, but she spent more time than she usually did with Barlowe so she could keep her eyes on Arya. She was the one who claimed to actually have talked to Cromwell, and Nikki didn't trust her. However, Nikki knew better than to come out and accuse her when she had no proof. She assumed that someone else was involved with Arya. Therefore, Nikki resolved herself to watch and wait in the hope that Arya would do or say something that would expose the truth.

Nikki had sent Butch to Chicago to look for Cromwell a week ago, and he reported that in that time, he'd had plenty of leads, but no one that he'd spoken to had actually seen Cromwell in months.

"Come on home, Butchie," Nikki told her soldier.

"I'll let you know when my flight arrives," Butch said, and Nikki ended the call that day.

Now that he was back, Nikki assigned him a new task. "While everybody thinks you're still out of town, I need you to do something for me."

"What's that?"

"I need you to follow Arya. Stay outta sight, but I wanna know where she goes and who she talks to."

"You got it."

The following day, Nikki and Cairo were at the restaurant, which she decided to name Elixirs. They had arrived there early that morning to wait for the delivery of a new stove. It didn't arrive on time; however, the electrician had arrived to install it, so now he was waiting as well and getting paid by the hour.

Naomi had been there earlier in the day, but when the stove wasn't delivered, Nikki sent her to Paragon Carpet Wholesaler to pick up samples.

"I'm back," Naomi announced when she returned to Elixirs.

"Let's see what you have for us," Nikki said as Naomi sat down at the table with her and Cairo.

"Okay." She laid out the samples she'd gotten. "This one is School Zone blue. That's Special Memories coconut husk brown."

"I like that one," Nikki said.

"I do, too," Naomi cosigned.

"What's this one called?" Cairo asked.

"Let me see." Naomi glanced at the fact sheet that she had been given. "That is called City Limits Telegram brown, and the last one is Corner Cafe espresso."

"I like that one, too," Nikki said, looking over the samples. "Which you do you like, Cairo?"

"Me?"

"Yeah, you."

"I'm kinda feeling the City Limits."

"What do you think, Mommy?"

"I could get with that. What do you think, Nikki?"

"I'm kinda feeling it too."

"Then it's settled, City Limits Telegram brown it is," Naomi said as the delivery men arrived with the stove. "About time."

"For real." Nikki watched as they set it in place, and then the electrician did his work.

"I've got some more errands to run, so I'm gonna get outta here," Naomi said and gathered her things to leave.

"Thank you for coming, Mommy. As soon as he's done with the stove, we're gonna get outta here too," Nikki informed her as she walked alongside Naomi to the door.

"You two are welcome to come for dinner," she said at the door.

"What are you cooking?" Cairo asked.

"Oh, I don't know. What do you want for dinner, Cairo?" Naomi asked.

"Oh, I don't know. What do you feel like cooking?"

"Y'all could go around and around like that for hours," Nikki said.

"Well, what do you want to eat?"

"You could make your steak and shrimp stir-fry. That's always good," Nikki suggested.

"I can go for that," Cairo said.

"Steak and shrimp stir-fry it is," Naomi said. "See y'all later."

It was late in the afternoon when the electrician finished the installation and left Elixirs. Nikki locked up the restaurant and was about to walk to where they had parked the car when she realized that she had left her phone inside on the table.

"Hold up," Nikki said and turned to go back inside.

When she did, the sniper's bullet that was aimed at her heart ripped through the flesh in her left arm. Nikki went down from the impact of the blast.

Cairo took cover behind a car. "You okay?" he asked Nikki as he got out his gun.

She crawled next to him and took out her gun. "Yeah, I'm okay."

Cairo looked at Nikki's arm, then he peeked over the hood of the car. "Third-floor window," he shouted, raised up, and opened fire. He took cover immediately as the sniper fired a volley of bullets that bounced off the car in front of them and the wall behind. When the shooting stopped, Nikki and Cairo fired a few shots in the direction of the window, but the sniper was gone.

"I think he's gone," Cairo said. "We gotta get outta here. You need a doctor," he said as he helped her to the car.

"No. Take me to Tasheka's house."

Cairo drove them there so she could tend to Nikki's wound.

Chapter Thirty-five

When Nikki and Cairo arrived at Tasheka's house, she helped him get Nikki into the kitchen and laid her out on the table.

"Awe!" Nikki yelled when he all but dropped her on the kitchen table.

"I'm sorry. I'm sorry," Cairo said, wiping the lone tear from the corner of his eye.

Tasheka cleaned and dressed Nikki's gunshot wound. Fortunately for her, it was just a flesh wound, as the bullet went straight through.

"Now you and Butch are twins," Cairo pointed out since they had both been shot in the arm.

"Glad I'm right-handed, so I can still shoot," Nikki said.

"Who do you think did it?" Tasheka asked as she worked.

"I don't know. I got more enemies than I thought I did. What you think, Cairo?"

"Before last week, I would have said it was some of Garraway's people who hit us. Now, since you and him made peace, I have no clue."

"Neither do I," Nikki said and thought about it. "But there's no harm in asking, right?"

She took out her phone and made a call.

"Hello, Nikki."

"Hello, Mr. Garraway."

"This is an unexpected surprise. How are you doing?"

"I'm fine, sir. How are you doing today, sir?"

"Not too bad for an old man. So, tell me, to what do I owe the pleasure of your call?"

"If you have the time, I'd like to get together with you. There's something I'd like to discuss with you."

"I'm not doing anything in particular right now. Where do you want to meet?"

"Whatever is convenient for you."

"Tell you what." He paused. "I just sent you a text with my address. Come by the house, and we'll talk."

"Sounds good." Nikki checked her phone. "I got your text, and I'll see you in about an hour."

"See you when you get here," Garraway said, and Nikki ended the call before making another.

"Hey, Mommy."

"Hey. I'm just getting home, and I haven't gotten started yet."

"Me and Cairo are going to make a stop at Mr. Garraway's house on the way, so there's no rush."

"You be careful." Naomi paused. "You tell Duncan that I said hello."

"I will, Mommy. I'll call you when I'm on my way there."

"Okay, Nikki," Naomi said and hung up the phone.

After she changed into something more comfortable, Naomi went to the kitchen to start dinner. She had taken out the shrimp and was about to start slicing the steak when the doorbell rang. Naomi went to the door and looked at the monitor. A woman she didn't recognize was standing there.

"Can I help you?" Naomi said over the intercom.

"I'm sorry to bother you, Mrs. Marx. My name is Francine Chaput. I was a friend of your son. It's important that I speak to Nikki."

Naomi opened the door. "Nikki's not here right now, but I expect her sometime soon. You're welcome to come in and wait for her."

"Thank you, Mrs. Marx," Francine said and went inside to wait for Nikki.

Cairo followed the directions to the address that Nikki had received from Garraway, and they were surprised when they turned onto his street. Where Barlowe lived in a seven-bedroom house with a pool in a gated community, Garraway's place was a modest house in a cul-de-sac.

"Not what I was expecting," Cairo said as he stopped in front of the house.

"Me either."

When they got out of the car and rang the bell, Cairo looked around the outside of the house for any signs of security. There was none. Nikki smiled when the door opened, and Capria Reynolds stood there with a welcoming smile on her face.

"Hi. You must be Nikki."

"Yes."

"I'm Capria, a friend of Mr. Garraway." She stepped aside. "Won't you please come in?"

"Thank you."

"Come this way, and I'll take you to Duncan."

Nikki and Cairo were escorted to the game room, where Garraway was waiting for them. He stood up when the door opened.

"Nikki!" Garraway said with his arms out.

"How are you, Mr. Garraway?"

"Doing fine, Nikki." He turned to Cairo with his hand out. "And you must be Cairo."

"Yes, sir." They shook hands.

"Good to meet you. Please, have a seat.

"Can I get you anything?" Capria asked as they took seats.

"No, thank you, we're fine."

"Then I will leave you to your business." Capria kissed Garraway on the cheek. "Let me know if you need anything."

"I will, Capria. Thank you," Garraway said, and Nikki was surprised when she left the room.

Arya would have planted herself whether she was invited or not, was Nikki's first thought.

"What can I do for you, Nikki?"

"Somebody tried to kill me again today. And before I did what I usually do, pick a target and retaliate, I thought that since we established this dialogue, I would take advantage of it."

"I'm glad you did. I can assure you that, to my knowledge, nobody in this camp had anything to do with it. I made it plain that whatever was going on with you and Wilkes is over. Of course, there are always some dead-enders who don't get the message. And if that's the case, I'll take care of it."

"I appreciate that."

"Like I said before, you are wise beyond your years, so I know that you are smart enough to know what is really going on here."

"Do I?"

"Stop me if I get off track," Garraway said, and Nikki nodded. "You found out that Wilkes had nothing to do with your brother's murder. So, you turned back to Cromwell. You've had your man in Chicago asking questions about him."

"How do you know that?"

"I have many friends, and your boy ain't subtle."

"That's Butch." Nikki giggled.

"I think the people involved are getting scared because you've seen through their diversion. See, they knew you would go hard at whoever you thought did it, and they aimed you like a gun at me. Now that you know I wasn't involved, they try to kill you to keep you from finding out the truth."

"That's right. That's exactly what I was thinking."

"The question is, what do you do now?"

"I stay on it. I've got my suspicions about who was involved, but I know she couldn't have done it alone, so I am waiting for her to expose herself."

"Arya?"

"You know her?"

"By reputation only. Never had the pleasure of meeting her."

"Trust me, you're not missing anything. She is the worst kind of snake."

"So I've been told," Garraway said as Nikki's phone rang. She took out her phone and glanced at the display.

"It's my mother. I need to take this," Nikki said and stood up.

"Tell Naomi that I said hello," Garraway said with a smile that showed the respect and admiration that he once had for her.

"Oh. I forgot to tell you. She said to tell you hello," Nikki said before she swiped the phone screen. "Hey, Mommy. What's up?"

"Sorry to bother you, but there's a Francine Chaput here who wants to see you. She said she's a friend of J.R.'s."

"Francine?" Nikki paused to think. "Did she say what she wanted?"

"No. Just that it was important that she speak to you."

"Okay, Mommy. I'm on my way." Nikki ended the call and turned to Garraway. "I gotta go."

Cairo stood up.

"If that is what I think it is, I may be about to hear what really happened," Nikki said.

Garraway stood up. "Then I hope that's what it is."

"Thank you for seeing me, Mr. Garraway," Nikki said with her hand out.

"This is what we opened the dialogue for."

"And I was hoping that one day, when you have the time, you might tell me more about my father."

"I would be honored."

"Thank you. We'll talk again soon," Nikki said, and Garraway escorted her and Cairo out.

On the way to her mother's house, Nikki speculated about what Francine wanted to talk to her about. Nobody had seen or heard from her since before J.R.'s funeral. Her absence at the funeral raised an eyebrow for Nikki, but at the time, it seemed a little unimportant. She assumed that Francine was too caught up in her grief to attend. However, Nikki knew that it was a safe bet that if Francine wanted to talk, she wanted to talk about Remy.

As soon as he walked into the house, Cairo could smell the steak and shrimp stir-fry. He exhaled. "That smells so good," Cairo said as he walked into the kitchen with Nikki.

Naomi was at the stove, and Francine was sitting at the table. She had dyed her hair red, and it was short, like a bob, a radical departure from the long black hair that hung down her back the last time Nikki saw her.

"Hey, Mommy."

"Good, you're here. Right on time for dinner."

Cairo sat down quickly, and Naomi began serving him. Nikki smiled because her mother liked having a man to cook for.

She sat next to Francine. "How are you, Francine?"

"I'm all right, Nikki. I'm sorry to just show up here like this, but I had to talk to you before I went back to Atlanta."

"Atlanta?"

"I've been down there since I left here."

"You have some dinner, Francine?" Naomi asked.

"No, thank you, Mrs. Marx. I'm gonna go after I talk to Nikki."

"It's a long drive to Atlanta. You might as well eat something before you get on the road."

Francine thought about it. "Okay, Mrs. Marx. I'll have a small plate."

"Why did you leave, Francine?" Nikki asked as Naomi served stir-fry to Francine, and then she made a plate for Nikki and herself.

"When I came home one day. I overheard Remy planning to kill J.R."

Nikki's anger swelled. "What did you hear him say?"

"I heard him say. 'she's gonna get Barlowe to send J.R. to collect some money from Cromwell, but it's a trap.'"

"I need to know who was in it with him. Did he say who she was?" Nikki asked, even though she had a good idea.

"No, he didn't. But whoever it was, she was the one that sent him pictures of me and J.R. together. When I asked him about it, Remy grabbed me by my hair and slapped me. He threatened to kill me, and I ran out the back door. I made it to my car and locked the door. Remy made it there. He began banging on the window, screaming for me to open the door. My hands were shaking. I'd never been so scared in my life. I put the car in reverse and drove away from there."

"I'm glad that you got out of there," Naomi said.

"I didn't stop driving until I was in Maryland. I stopped for gas and kept going to Atlanta. I've got a girlfriend there that I went to college with. I've been staying with her ever since."

"Why'd you come back?" Nikki asked.

Francine wiped away her tears. "I came back because I got a job, and I needed to get some documents from the Department of Health. But I knew I had to come here and tell you what I knew." Her tears began to flow again. "I tried to call J.R. to warn him while I was on the road, but he didn't answer. I didn't know how to get in touch with either of you. When I got to Atlanta and called again, it went straight to voicemail. It was a couple of days later when I heard he was dead," she cried. "I'm so sorry."

"It's okay, Francine," Nikki said, patting her on the back to comfort her.

"I'm sorry, Mrs. Marx." Francine bounced out of her seat. "I have to go."

"I understand," Naomi said, and she followed Francine to the door. "You drive safely, child, and thank you for coming to tell us this. I can't tell you how much this means to us."

Francine didn't say anything. She just rushed to her car, crying, and got in. Naomi watched her drive away before she went back inside.

"It was Remy," Nikki said as soon as Naomi came back into the kitchen. "And there is no doubt in my mind that the 'she' Francine was talking about was Arya."

"Can't be nobody but. I mean, who else could get Barlowe to send J.R. to collect?" Cairo asked.

"And Barlowe never talked to Cromwell himself. That was Arya, too," Nikki stated.

Naomi sat down at the table. "What are you gonna do?"

"I'm gonna kill them all for what they did."

Chapter Thirty-six

After they finished eating, Nikki and Cairo left her mother's house. He thought she'd want to drive to Remy's house to kill him. Nikki had other ideas.

"We need to take our time on this one. Especially if I'm right and Arya's involved in it with him."

"So, what you wanna do?"

"Call Butchie and tell him to meet us at y'all's crib."

"On it," Cairo said, taking out his phone to make the call.

When they arrived at the apartment, Butch was there waiting for them. Nikki brought him up to speed on what they had found out from Francine. And then Butch dropped a bit of information.

"That makes sense because I followed Arya to the Ludlow Hotel. She met Remy there."

"I knew it!" Nikki exclaimed.

"You were right. That bitch is in it with him," Cairo said as Rah-Rah came out of Butch's bedroom, naked.

"Oh, sorry, Nikki. I didn't know you were here."

Nikki pointed at Rah-Rah. "She still here?"

"I told you what's up with that," Cairo said.

"Yeah, yeah, house pussy. You told me." Nikki shook her head. She thought for a while and looked at Rah-Rah. "You know what?"

"What?" Butch asked.

"I'm gonna do her a favor."

"What's that?" Cairo asked.

"I've seen this movie before, so I know what's gonna happen to her. Y'all gonna let her smoke and fuck her until she burns herself out. Then, when she gets skinny and don't wanna bathe no more, y'all will put her out on the street and get you a new one."

Cairo and Butch looked at one another. "Yeah," they said in unison.

"Yeah, well, not this time. So, like I said, I'm gonna do her a favor."

"What's that?"

"I'm taking her to rehab."

"Rehab?" Butch questioned.

"Yes, Butch. I'm taking Rah-Rah to rehab." Nikki looked at Rah-Rah. "Get dressed, Rah-Rah. I'm taking you to rehab before you burn yourself out."

"You think I need that, Nikki?" Rah-Rah asked, and everyone just looked at her.

"Look at her. Mind's already gone." Nikki walked over to her. "Yes, Rah-Rah. I think you need to be in rehab."

"Okay, Nikki. If you think that's what's best."

"You go put some clothes on so we can leave," Nikki said, and once again, Cairo and Butch looked at each other.

"What?"

"She doesn't have any clothes," Butch said.

"What?"

"She doesn't have any clothes," Butch repeated.

"Why not?" Nikki needed to know.

"Because she ruined the clothes she had in the washing machine."

"You're kidding."

"No kidding," Cairo said.

"Find her something to wear so we can go, please."

"Come on, Rah-Rah," Cairo said and led her into his room.

While Nikki looked up rehabilitation facilities, Cairo got some sweatpants and an oversized shirt for Rah-Rah to wear. Once she was dressed, they took Rah-Rah to Northwell Health at South Oaks Hospital, an inpatient detoxification treatment center on Sunrise Highway in Amityville. Nikki paid cash, and she was admitted.

"That was my good deed for the day," Nikki said as they were walking back to the car.

"Yeah, but now we gotta find us some new house pussy," Butch said as they got in the car.

"That shouldn't be a problem for you two," Nikki said.

"It won't be. But I kinda liked Rah-Rah," Cairo said as Butch drove away from Northwell.

"Maybe you couldn't have turned her out," Nikki said. "Ain't nobody stopping you from going to see her while she's in rehab. But right now, we got work to do."

"So, we going to kill these muthafuckas now, or what?" Butch asked.

"Not yet. Like I said, with Arya being involved, I wanna take my time, set this thing up and do it right."

"So, what do you want us to do?"

"Drop me off at my mom's house, and then you get back on following Arya, Butch. Cairo, I wanted you to follow Remy. I wanna know what you think is gonna be the best way to hit him without drawing too many of his people into it. Understood?"

"Understood."

The following night, Nikki was at the Palace in the office, talking to Megan, when Cairo and Butch arrived.

"Can I get you something to drink?"

"Thank you, Megan," Cairo said, and he went to sit down. That was when they heard the noise coming from the club.

Megan bounced up, "Is that shooting I hear?"

"Sounds like it." Cairo stood up. "You really do need to hire more and better security for this place, Megan."

"Recruiting people to get shot at hasn't been easy. But I'm open to suggestions."

When Cairo took out his gun, so did Nikki and Butch. They started for the door.

"Stay here, Megan," Nikki said.

"If you insist." Megan armed herself and went to hide under the desk. She aimed her weapon at the door.

When Nikki, Cairo, and Butch came out of the office, customers were hitting the floor or taking cover under the tables while others were running for the exits, trying to get out. As the customers and staff attempted to make it to some semblance of safety, they saw two men with automatic weapons standing on either side of the bar. Nikki, Cairo, and Butch began firing at them, and the men ran.

Just then, one man stepped into the club armed with a semi-automatic weapon and opened fire. Nikki, Cairo, and Butch immediately sought better cover together as two more men rushed in with semi-automatic weapons and began firing. All the gunmen sprayed the area with bullets. As the gunmen fired, Cairo stayed low and moved to get a better angle on the shooter. Nikki crawled along the floor to make it to a spot where she could get a clear shot. Then she stood, fired, and then dove for the ground. Nikki raised her weapon and shot one in the head. When he went down, Cairo fired and took out the second gunman. Butch raised up, aimed his weapon, and opened fire, hitting the last of the gunmen.

With the big guns down and the club all but empty of civilians, Cairo quickly turned over a table for cover, and then he and Butch opened fire on the remaining gunmen. Cairo and Butch kept shooting as one of the gunmen stopped firing to reload. Cairo stood up and hit him with two shots to the chest. The gunman went down, and Butch took aim and shot another gunman.

Now, only one of the gunmen remained, and he tried to make it out of there. While the gunman sprayed the area with bullets, Nikki kept firing, while Butch made a move to get behind him. With the shooter's attention focused on Cairo, Butch was able to put his gun to the back of his head, and he pulled the trigger.

"Everybody all right?" Nikki asked her men.

"I'm good," Cairo said.

Nikki looked around the club for fallen civilians. She didn't see any at first glance, but as intense as the firefight had been, Nikki was sure there would be civilian casualties. There were always one or two at these shootouts. Silence about what any witnesses saw and may have heard could be taken care of with money. Those who thought about talking to the cops regretted it and quickly changed their stories. "I didn't see a thing" became the story no matter what they'd said in statements previously.

"Me too," Butch said, reloading his weapon as they walked around.

"You recognized any of them?" Nikki asked.

"I don't," Butch said.

"Neither do I," Cairo said.

"They gonna keep coming at us until we end this thing," Butch said. "I say we end it."

"Yeah, I know. And I'm not disagreeing with you, because you're right. They are gonna keep coming. So, tell me, Cairo, what's the best way to hit Remy without causing a war with his people?" Nikki asked, and Cairo laid out his plan for her.

"I like it," Nikki said.

"We're gonna need to kill Jace and Hakeem first," Butch added.

"All part of the plan, my nigga," Cairo said.

"What about Arya?" Butch asked. "How do you wanna handle her?"

"Oh, I'm just gonna walk up to her and put two bullets in her head the second I see her snake ass."

"What about Barlowe? How you think he's gonna feel about you killing his boo?"

"I really don't give a fuck. If he doesn't like it, he can get killed right along with her," Nikki said, thinking about him killing her father and trying to rape her mother. "He might get his anyway. I haven't decided yet."

At some point, Barlowe would have to answer for what he'd done.

"Whatever you decide, Nikki, I'm down with you," Cairo said.

"Me too," Butch cosigned. "Ride or die. Bad boys down with you for life," Butch said.

"Just don't start singing that damn song," Nikki said on her way back to the office.

When they came into the office, Megan had come out from hiding under the desk and was seated at it. When the door opened, Megan pointed her gun at Nikki, Cairo, and Butch.

Nikki froze and put up her hands. "Ease off, Megan. It's just us."

She lowered the weapon. "Just making sure." Megan laughed. "Can't be too careful. We are at war, you know."

"I know."

Chapter Thirty-seven

It took a week to go down, but that morning, Ladonna Marco was awakened by the sound of someone ringing her doorbell. She was the manager at Le Bistro Urbain, Remy's New Orleans-themed French restaurant. When she ignored the ringing, they started banging on her door.

"Shit!" she shouted, sitting up in bed.

As the banging continued, Ladonna sat on the edge of the bed. She looked at her clock. It was seven forty-five. Ladonna had worked late the night before and didn't get in bed until well after three. She wondered who it could be at that hour of the morning and stood up. She liked to sleep naked, so she put on her Kate Spade New York robe and went to the door.

"Who is it?" she shouted as she got close to the door.

"It's Nikki Marx!"

Ladonna stopped in her tracks. "What do you want?"

"I want to talk to you, Ladonna. Can I come in?"

Ladonna got to the door and glanced out the peephole. She saw Nikki standing there but couldn't tell if she was alone. "Just a minute," she said before she opened the door.

"Thank you, Ladonna," Nikki said as she came into the apartment. "I'm sorry to bother you so early in the morning, but it is critical that I talk to you."

"Come in and have a seat," Ladonna said, leading Nikki into the living room. "I need coffee. Do you want some?"

"That would be nice. Thank you," Nikki said and sat down.

Ladonna put on a pot of coffee, and then she came into the living room and sat across from Nikki. "What did you want to talk about, Nikki?"

"The future."

Ladonna let out a little laugh. "The future?"

"Yes, Ladonna, the future. Your future."

"Okay," Ladonna said slowly and tentatively.

"J.R. told me that you were smart and that you were ambitious. Is that true?" Nikki leaned forward. "Are you smart and ambitious?"

"I like to think that I am."

"Good. You have to believe in yourself if you're gonna get people to believe in you."

"I agree." Ladonna stood up. "I'll be right back."

Nikki smiled. "Take your time."

"How do you like your coffee?"

"Black is fine," Nikki said as Ladonna went into the kitchen. As she poured the coffee, she was even more curious about what Nikki wanted.

The future. What is she talking about? she asked herself. *Whatever she wants, it's important enough for her to show up here at the crack of dawn.*

Ladonna went back into the living room and handed Nikki her coffee.

"Thank you."

She sat down, knowing that Nikki Marx was a dangerous woman, and whatever she wanted, it would be in her best interests to do what she said.

"Let's talk about the future," said Ladonna.

"There are going to be a lot of changes in the organization."

"What kind of changes?"

"New people in new positions."

"I see."

"What I need to know from you is if I can count on you to be a part of that future I'm building."

"Yes. I want to be a part of whatever future you're building."

"That's good to hear." Nikki sipped her coffee. "J.R. said you were smart and ambitious, but are you loyal? Can I depend on your loyalty to me?"

"Yes, Nikki. You can trust me to be loyal to you."

Ladonna knew then that she was about to be asked to betray Remy, and she thought briefly about how she felt about that. She had worked for Remy for a long time. And, in the time that she had worked for him, she thought he was an arrogant asshole who was disrespectful to the women who worked for him. She thought he talked to them like they were stupid. Although he hadn't disrespected her, Ladonna had come to grips with the fact that, eventually, he would say something insulting to her as well.

But is that a reason to betray him?

She looked at Nikki and assumed that Remy was going to die.

Me staying alive is a reason to betray him.

"What do you need me to do?"

Later that evening at Le Bistro Urbain, Ladonna was getting set up for the dinner rush when Remy came into the restaurant with Jace and Hakeem. She watched as Remy went to the office, and Jace and Hakeem took up their usual positions at the bar. Ladonna took out her phone and sent a text message.

They're here.

Cairo looked at the message and then at his watch. "Right on time." If his plan were to work, the timing was crucial.

We're ready.

When Ladonna got the reply, she went to the bar where Jace and Hakeem were drinking. "I got some stuff in my car that I need some help bringing in. Can you two help me?"

"Of course we can," Jace said and shot his drink. Hakeen stood up, and they followed Ladonna through Le Bistro Urbain to the back door. When they stepped outside, Cairo and Butch were standing there.

"What's poppin'?" Cairo asked, and Butch shot them both in the head.

"Damn," Ladonna said and looked away.

Once again, Cairo glanced at his watch. He nodded and looked at Ladonna. "You go on back inside and be ready."

He didn't have to tell her twice. Ladonna quickly grabbed the handle and rushed inside. She leaned against the door and exhaled. Once she had composed herself, Ladonna stood and returned to the restaurant to wait.

Meanwhile, outside behind the restaurant, Cairo and Butch picked up Jace and Hakeem's bodies and carried them to the dumpster. They put the bodies in and closed the lid.

Cairo looked at his watch.

"Okay. Where they at?" Butch asked.

"Should be any minute now," Cairo said as a front-load garbage truck turned down the alley behind the restaurant. He pointed. "Right on time."

Cairo and Butch stood back and watched the truck stop, pick up, and then empty the dumpster into the truck. They waited and watched while the trash was compacted before the truck pulled off.

"So much for Jace and Hakeem," Cairo said and fist-bumped Butch.

A few minutes later, Nikki walked into the entrance at Le Bistro Urbain and allowed herself to be seated by the wait staff. When she nodded at Ladonna, she approached the table.

"Welcome back to Le Bistro Urbain, Nikki."

"Evening, Ladonna. Please tell Remy that Nikki Marx is here to see him."

"No problem. Wait here, and I'll get him," Ladonna said, and she headed for the office.

When she was out of sight, Nikki stood up and followed her to the office. Ladonna knocked on Remy's office door.

"Come in!" Remy shouted.

Ladonna peeked her head inside the office. "Nikki Marx is here to see you."

"Okay. Tell her I'll be right out," he said, and Ladonna closed the door.

Remy stood up, came from behind his desk, and opened the door. Nikki and Cairo were standing there. He had his gun pointed at Remy.

"Sup?" Cairo asked as Butch came up behind Remy.

He covered Remy's mouth with a rag soaked in chloroform. Cairo and Butch grabbed Remy's body before it hit the floor. They carried him out the back door.

"Le Bistro Urbain is yours, Ladonna," Nikki told her. Then she followed Cairo and Butch out the back door.

Ladonna smiled as she watched the door close, and then she went into the office and sat behind the desk. She looked around what was now her office, thinking about the future.

Cairo and Butch put Remy's body into the trunk of their car, and they drove to Elixirs. They spread drop cloths in the middle of the floor, and then they brought Remy in. Once they tied him to a chair, Nikki stood up and walked toward him.

"Wake him up," she said, and Butch threw a bucket of cold water on him.

"Shit!" Remy shouted and tried to shake it off. That's when he realized that he was tied to the chair. He struggled against his bonds.

"What's this about, Nikki?" he shouted angrily.

"It's time for you to answer for J.R.," Nikki said.

"J.R.? Fuck is you talking about?"

"You know exactly what I'm talking about." Nikki got a chair and pulled it up in front of Remy. She sat down. "I never liked you, Remy, but I respected you. If you said it, you did it. I respected that. So I . . . foolishly . . . thought that you would say, 'yeah, I had J.R. killed.'"

Nikki looked at Butch and Cairo. "Foolish, right?"

The three of them laughed, but not Remy.

"Since you wanna play stupid, stop me if I get any of this wrong." Nikki leaned forward. "You found out that J.R. was fucking Francine. Someone sent you pictures of them together, and you decided to kill them. But you're a fuckin' coward, so you needed somebody to take the heat. Who better than Cromwell?"

Cairo got in Remy's face to say, "Since he's dead and shit."

"I was gonna say that." Nikki laughed. "Anyway, you got Arya to tell Barlowe that Cromwell had his money, and he sent my brother into your trap. I get any of that wrong?"

Remy said nothing.

"Nothing to say, huh? That's all right." Nikki stood up. "I was gonna let Cairo and Butch take turns beating you until you admitted what you did, but I changed my mind."

"I was looking forward to beating your ass," Cairo said.

"What you gonna do instead, Nikki?" Butch wanted to know.

"Where's his gun?" Nikki asked, and Cairo handed her the gun.

"Thank you."

"No problem," Cairo said as Nikki stepped up to Remy, pointed the gun at his kneecap, and pulled the trigger.

Remy screamed in pain. "Shit!" he said through gritted teeth.

"Say it!" Nikki shot him in the other kneecap.

"Fuck you!" Remy shouted.

"Say it!" Nikki shot him in the thigh.

Remy screamed again. "Just kill me and get it over with!"

"No. You need to feel this pain, muthafucka," Nikki said, and she shot him in the other thigh.

"The nuts are next," Butch said, laughing.

"Oh, no, not the nuts!" Cairo shouted, and he laughed.

"Say it!"

"Go to hell!"

"Right." Nikki raised the gun to Remy's temple and shot him in the head.

Butch laughed. "I thought you were gonna say something cool like, 'you first,'" he said.

"Get him outta here."

Chapter Thirty-eight

Cairo and Butch wrapped Remy's body in the drop cloth and took him out the back door of Elixir. They loaded the body in the trunk of the car and got in with Nikki. They drove to one of Barlowe's construction sites, parked, and got out.

"We haven't got much time," Nikki said.

Cairo and Butch got shovels out of the trunk, and the three walked into the building.

"This is a good spot," Nikki said, pointing to a spot on the ground.

While Nikki looked out, Cairo and Butch dug a hole in the ground. Once they had dug the hole deep enough, they went back to their car and got Remy's body out of the trunk. They carried the body back into the building and threw it in the hole they'd dug. They covered the body and filled the hole. Then they made the ground look as if it hadn't been disturbed before they headed back to the car.

"They're gonna lay concrete in the morning," Nikki said as Butch drove away.

"It will be decades, if ever, before the body is found," Cairo said.

"What now, Nikki?" Butch asked.

She glanced at the clock on the dashboard. "That's it for tonight. We'll settle things with Arya and Barlowe tomorrow."

"You want me to take you to your mom's house?"

"Yeah. Then y'all go home and get some rest."

"Home ain't gonna be as much fun as it used to be," Butch said.

"What you mean?" Nikki asked.

"You sent Rah-Rah away. No more house pussy," Cairo said.

"You'll get over it." Nikki laughed. "And probably have some new house pussy up in there tomorrow."

"True that. But I kinda liked Rah-Rah," Cairo said.

"Then maybe you shouldn't have burnt her out," Nikki said. She relaxed in her seat for the ride to her mother's house.

Talk of Remy's disappearance didn't take long to spread. Ladonna was inundated with questions about what happened to Remy.

"All I know is one minute he was in his office, and nobody has seen him since."

"Maybe he left with Nikki?" one of her employees asked.

"No. I saw Nikki leave when I couldn't find Remy," was Ladonna's answer.

She was in charge of Le Bistro Urbain, and her mind was set on being a part of the future that Nikki spoke of.

By mid-afternoon, the word of Remy's disappearance had reached Barlowe. He was at the house with Arya. It was apparent that the news had shaken her, and that left him to wonder why. It made him think back to something that Nikki said to him: *I know that's your woman, but if her lips are moving, she's telling a lie. Everybody sees that but you.* His answer had been that Arya served a purpose, but he had to admit that there were some days when he wondered what that purpose was and who benefited from it.

That afternoon, Barlowe and Arya were in the living room watching television when Nikki arrived at the house with Cairo and Butch.

"Nikki is here to see you."

"Bring her in," Barlowe said.

"I'm really not in the mood for any of Nikki's nonsense," Arya said.

Barlowe said nothing as Nikki came into the room with Cairo and Butch.

"Hey, Nikki," Barlowe said.

She didn't say a word. Nikki went and picked up the remote control and turned off the television.

"What the fuck," Arya barked.

"What are you doing?" Barlowe asked.

"Time to settle some old scores," Nikki said.

"What are you talking about?" Barlowe asked.

Nikki looked at Arya. "It's way past time for you to answer for J.R."

"What are you talking about, Nikki?" Barlowe asked, but Arya said nothing.

"She knows," Cairo said.

"She knows what?" Barlowe asked.

"Remy is dead, Arya," Nikki began. "I killed him."

"What?" Barlowe questioned. "Why?"

"Arya sent Remy pictures of J.R. and Francine. That set Remy off, and he decided to kill J.R."

"Over some pussy," Butch said.

"So Remy and this bitch come up with a scheme, and she tells you that Cromwell is ready to pay what he owes. But Cromwell is dead. He OD'ed somewhere in Milwaukee. All that so you'd send J.R. to collect."

"She's lying!" Arya shouted.

Nikki raised her gun and shot Arya in the head. "No. I'm not lying."

Barlowe was shaken, but he did his best not to show it. He looked at Arya's body on the floor. "It had to be done," he said.

"I'm glad you understand that it had to be done," Nikki said and went to sit across from Barlowe.

As Cairo and Butch removed Arya's body from the room, she crossed her legs and placed her gun on her lap. "But I said that I was here to settle some old scores."

"What do you mean?"

"It's time for you to answer for my father."

Barlowe took a deep breath and exhaled. "What did Garraway tell you?"

"The truth."

"I'm sorry, Nikki," Barlowe said with a hint of resignation in his voice.

"You're sorry? You tried to rape my mother, and you had my father killed, and you're sorry."

"Yes, Nikki. I'm sorry. I was mad and humiliated after Eddie left that night. He threatened to kill me, and I made the call. I regretted it the minute I set it in motion. I tried to stop it, but you know how these things go. It was too late to stop it."

"Fuck that!" Nikki raised her weapon. "You could have warned him!" she shouted.

"I tried. God knows I tried. I called him, but he wouldn't take my calls. I called the house, but Naomi hung up on me."

"You tried to rape her!"

"I know what I did!" Barlowe shouted. "Nobody knows what I did better than me. I had my best friend killed! I have to live with that fact every day. Every time I look in the mirror, I'm reminded that I ordered my best friend's murder. All I could do was try to make up for it."

"I always wondered why Mommy hated you so much. Never could understand it because you had been so good to us."

"Now you know that I deserved every bit of that hatred."

"And now you're gonna die for it," Nikki said and stood up.

"Tell your mother that I'm sorry," Barlowe said before Nikki raised her weapon and shot him twice in the head.

Chapter Thirty-nine

Peace. It was a long time coming, but now that it was here, it was welcome. When Nikki woke up that morning, all of her enemies were dead. Remy, Arya, and Barlowe were dead. Nikki killed them all. She had avenged the deaths of her brother and her father.

After she'd taken care of Barlowe and Arya, Nikki had called a cleaner to dispose of the bodies.

"What now?" Cairo asked.

"Now we build," Nikki said, thinking about the plans that she had for the future.

"The new world according to Nikki Marx," Butch said as he pulled into the driveway at her mother's house.

"What time do you want us to come get you in the morning?" Cairo asked as Nikki got out.

"I'll call you and let you know."

"Are you ever gonna stay in your own place?"

"I was thinking about selling it."

"Don't do that," Cairo said quickly.

"Why? Y'all wanna move in there?"

"Shit, yeah," Butch said. "Your building is the shit."

"Not to mention all the fine-ass women that live in your building," Cairo added. "And access to a new clientele. Shit, yeah."

"Done." Nikki tossed the keys to her condo and shut the car door. "See you in the morning."

When she went into the house, Naomi was still awake. She was sitting in the living room. "Hey, Nikki."

"What are you still doing up?"

"I couldn't sleep, so I got up and made myself a drink."

"Is it helping you sleep?"

"Not really."

"Well, what are you drinking?"

Naomi raised her glass. "Vodka and orange juice."

Nikki went and got the bottle. "Mind if I join you?"

"Not at all."

"There's something I need to tell you," Nikki said as she poured.

"Is it gonna put me to sleep?" Naomi giggled.

"Probably not. But it may allow you to rest easier."

"I'm for that." Naomi took a sip of her drink. "What do you want to tell me?"

"Pete Barlowe is dead."

Naomi smiled a delighted smile. "How did he die?"

"I killed him."

"I knew once you found out about what happened, that's what was going to happen." Naomi raised her glass. "May he rest in peace. The bastard. I'm glad he's dead. I only wish I had been there to watch the bastard take his last breath."

"He said to tell you that he was sorry."

"Fuck him. Sorry doesn't make up for all that he took from me. All he took from us."

"I know, Mommy."

"I knew he did all he did out of a guilty conscience. I understood that, and I did my best not to let my hate affect the relationship he had with you kids."

"I know I wouldn't be who I am if it weren't for him. I learned a lot from him." Nikki laughed. "Even if it was for all the wrong reasons."

"And they were the wrong reasons, but you're right. No matter how I felt about him, he did right by us."

"He felt like he owed it to us."

"Because he did. He took everything from me that day. The flashbacks, nightmares, weeks and months of depression." Naomi shook her head. "I can't tell you how many times I thought about committing suicide."

"I can't even imagine what you must have been feeling."

"I wouldn't wish those feelings on anybody. I blamed myself for allowing it to happen."

"It wasn't your fault."

"For the longest time, I felt damaged and unworthy. I felt so vulnerable, and I was always afraid." Naomi finished her drink. "Afraid for you kids. Not so much for myself. I wanted to die most days, but I was afraid he would do something to hurt you kids if I said a word to anyone."

"And we were so naive."

"Especially your brother," Naomi said and stood up to make herself another drink. "J.R. thought the world of Pete."

"Worshipped the ground he walked on," Nikki added.

"You did, too." Naomi returned to her seat and took a sip. "What changed your mind about Pete anyway?"

"Years of listening to you." Nikki laughed. "J.R. would always say, 'that's Mommy talking.' And it was. But after a while, I saw how he was using us like his own personal attack dogs."

"As I remember, you were all into it at one time."

"I was. There is nothing in the world more intoxicating than power and money. Especially being as young as I was. I couldn't get enough of the life. But then I opened my eyes."

"You had to see for yourself. All I did was lead you to the water and hoped that one day you'd be thirsty enough to drink."

"Anyway. Something else I need to tell you."

"What's that? You found out who had your brother murdered?"

"I did."

"Who?"

"Arya was in it with Remy."

"I thought so. That bitch."

"Remy and Arya set him up."

"I never trusted that bitch."

"With good reason. They're both dead, too."

"Damn, daughter. You had quite a day, didn't you?"

"I settled all of our family's business."

Nikki finished her drink and stood up. "And now I'm going to bed."

Nikki kissed her mother. "Good night, Mommy."

"Good night, Nikki. Tomorrow, I'll make you something special for breakfast."

"Thank you, Mommy," Nikki said, and she went up to her room to sleep.

The following morning, Naomi was up early to cook. By the time Nikki came dragging into the kitchen, she had prepared her famous bacon crunch wrap casserole, bacon-and-cheddar grits quiche, and grilled steak strips.

"Morning, Mommy," Nikki said and got her coffee cup.

"Morning."

"All this food, Mommy."

"Okay, so l got a little carried away," Naomi said as Nikki sat down and took out her phone.

"Sup, Nik-Nik?" Butch asked when he answered.

"Y'all come eat. Mommy made enough food to feed an army."

"We are on our way."

"Hurry up." Nikki helped herself to the selections Naomi had set out for her.

It was about fifteen minutes later when the doorbell rang. "That was fast," Nikki said as she was about to get up to answer the door.

"You go ahead and eat. I'll get the door," Naomi said and went to the door.

Thinking that it was Cairo and Butch, Naomi opened the door without looking.

"Hello, Naomi."

"Clarence?"

"Yes, Naomi, it's me."

"What are you doing here?"

"I came to see you and Nikki. Is she here?"

"Yes, but that still doesn't explain what you're doing here."

"Barlowe is dead, so we have a lot to discuss. Can I come in?"

"I'm sorry." Naomi held the door open. "Please come in," she said to Clarence Cunningham. He had been Pete Barlowe's lawyer for the last twenty years.

"Thank you. I was going to send a courier to invite you to my office to read Pete's will, but then I thought that I hadn't seen you in fourteen years."

"Has it been that long?" Naomi asked, even though she clearly remembered the last time she saw him.

"It was shortly after Eddie passed."

"Oh, yes," Naomi said and led him into the kitchen. "Nikki, this is Clarence Cunningham. He's Pete Barlowe's lawyer."

"I've seen you at the house a few times," Nikki said. "Good to finally meet you."

"Same here. I'm so sorry to have interrupted your breakfast."

"You're more than welcome to have some," Naomi said.

"I wouldn't want to intrude."

"Nonsense. She made plenty." Nikki laughed. "Enough to feed an army."

"Okay. You talked me into it," he said and sat down. Naomi placed a plate in front of him.

"Don't be shy. Help yourself," Naomi said.

"Thank you," Clarence said and began filling his plate.

"So, Mr. Cunningham. What can I do for you?"

"As I was telling your mother, with Pete being dead, I'm here to settle his estate."

"His estate?" Nikki questioned.

"Yes. His estate, Nikki. The property, the money."

"He left something to me?"

"He left everything to you, Nikki. Well, you and J.R., but since he's no longer with us, it all belongs to you. The houses he owned and a sizable amount of money in stocks and other investments, all yours."

"What about this house?" Naomi asked.

"What do you mean?"

"Did he leave Nikki this house?"

"You've owned this house free and clear since Mr. Marx died, Naomi."

"Excuse me?"

"When Eddie died, Pete paid for the house."

"I knew that," Nikki said. "He used to remind me of that fact all the time."

"What he didn't tell you was that he filed a quick claim deed in Naomi's name. The house has been yours for years, Naomi."

"What about the clubs? The Palace, XL, and Marquee?" Nikki asked, and Clarence looked confused.

"I guess Barlowe didn't tell you that either."

"Tell me what?"

"That after your father passed, Pete set up a receivership and put the clubs under it. I can't believe he didn't tell you two any of this."

"I can believe it. The bastard didn't tell any of that to anybody. Not one word," Naomi said as the doorbell rang.

"That's probably Cairo and Butchie."

"I'll get it," Naomi said and went to the door to let them into the house to eat.

"So, how does it work?"

"The receivership?"

"Yes. How does it work?" she asked because Nikki had never heard of a receivership.

"A receivership is a legal process in which a court-appointed receiver—me. I manage the assets, operations, and finances."

"And?"

"When you turned eighteen, ownership of the three clubs and the construction business all became yours, Nikki. Same with J.R. However, as I said, with him having passed, it all belongs to you. I can't believe that Pete never mentioned any of this to you."

"What are we talking about?" Cairo asked as he sat down at the table with Butch.

"Barlowe left everything to Nikki," Naomi said.

"No shit," Cairo said and began filling his plate. "The clubs, everything?"

"Yup," Nikki said.

"Wow."

"Unexpected, but cool," Nikki said.

It took a couple of weeks to settle everything that Clarence spoke about, but when it was over, not only was Nikki on top, but she was also now a businesswoman. There was only one thing left on her agenda.

"Nikki!" Garraway said when he opened the door and saw her standing there.

"Hello, Mr. Garraway. I hope you don't mind me just stopping by like this."

"Not at all. Please come in."

"Thank you."

"Now, tell me what I can do for you."

"Tell me about my father."